MAIL ORDER MISTAKE

GINNY STERLING

THE REVIEWS HAVE IT...

The romance was excellent, trust and longing embedded into this romance. - Amazon Reviewer

Very enjoyable story and I liked that it was set in Canada for a change of pace. In addition, not knowing who the matchmaker is makes for a bit of mystery as to if the person will be revealed in one of the following stories. - Amazon Reviewer

Wonderful storyline. Interesting concept. These two make a wonderful couple. Ginny writes addicting stories. She keeps your interest peaked. Highly recommend!! - Amazon Reviewer

INTRODUCTION

There is magic in love…

Russell Wolfe was a victim of cholera, just like the others. Helpless, he witnessed first-hand as the disease wiped out both friend and foe, leaving him alone, bitter, and hostile, on the outskirts of this cursed town. When a secret matchmaker sends out a plea for help to bring hope and a fresh start to Lore Valley, Russell finds himself face to face with a bride he never expected and can't find the strength to turn away.

For Rose Bonnett, this was just another mistake in a long line of screw-ups in her life. Cursing her stubbornness, she refused to ask for help because it always seemed to backfire right in her face. Answering the tempting ad in the paper, she was whisked to the middle of a small town that was left reeling from the onslaught of unexpected brides arriving suddenly.

Hadn't Lore Valley planned for this plethora of eligible young women? Why were they so amused at the fact that Rose was matched with Russell? Could this 'curse' truly be a 'blessing in disguise' after all?

A sweet and clean romance Mail-Order Bride series that can be read together or individually with a Happily Ever After that is legendary...

For my lovely Readers
You make me smile

Sign up for updates and notifications

CHAPTER 1

"THIS MAKES NO SENSE," ROSE REPEATED STUBBORNLY, looking around at the bevy of eligible women on the train car that were all coming to the same horrible conclusion. She was on a train with a variety of women that had come from miles and miles away. Some smiled, some looked concerned, and a few looked quite peeved as the same realization dawned on them... all at once.

This was a setup... a prank... a sick joke.

How could one small town in the middle of nowhere suddenly need so many mail-order brides? Was there some disastrous plague that wiped out the women of town? Were they to be marrying men whose wives had died off because of old age—or perhaps they were smart enough to jump ship while they could, running away from a pack of hideous monsters while they could?

They didn't even have names of their prospective grooms! It was all done in a way that piqued her curiosity, and fear drove her the rest of the way there, combined with a desperate hope and clinging to a prayer. Rose loved intrigue and had a stubborn streak a mile wide, landing her where she was now. Lost, alone, and possibly making another careless mistake for the sake of adventure.

Growing up, she'd been a burden to her family with her adventurous ways for as long as she could remember. Her mother had repeated fits of the vapors at her multiple attempts to dress as a boy—one of which started with a shorn head that took forever to grow out.

How could she *not* want to be a boy?

Boys had so much more freedom and got away with everything… where she had to be proper, she had to behave, and exude grace in whatever she did. Boys were praised for their hunting skills, their prowess in cards, and as they grew —they were then applauded for some of the seedier things they did.

Boys thrived at the chance for adventure, and yet, girls were supposed to shun it? That didn't sit right with Rose…

Another time, middle of the summer, she refused to wear a dress, insisting that her chemise was the newest fashion from Paris. Her father turned three different shades of red before he started shouting about his '*heathen child*'. It was hot, and they didn't seem to understand just how warm all those terribly bulky all layers could be!

Rose was anything but graceful or ladylike.

She was more like a whirlwind, doing *what* she wanted, *when* she wanted—and because of that she'd jumped at the chance to begin a new adventure in a town. A new environment and group of people that didn't avoid her like the plague… fearing that being bold would be contagious.

Women avoided her, afraid to talk to the wild, wanton woman that acted out of character. Men steered away for fear that they wouldn't make a respectable marriage if they were seen talking with Rose. Yes, she needed a fresh start, and this was the perfect opportunity.

The ad in the paper had been incredibly tempting, hitting every little nugget of desire within her. She re-read the post several times before replying—and once her mind was made up? She was practically on her way!

Looking for a fresh start? Yearning for new horizons?
Perhaps a little freedom and adventure is just what you need
— well, it's waiting for you! A village rich in trade and ripe with
opportunity, Lore Valley will make all your fondest wishes come
true. Become a legendary bride, cherished and treasured beyond
belief.
Time is short—embrace your destiny!

"Do you think that perhaps the people were set upon by pirates, marauders, or maybe Indians?" Penelope asked softly; her bright green eyes widened perceptibly and Rose arched an eyebrow at the woman. She couldn't tell if Penelope was happy or upset about the idea of trouble being there before they even arrived. Maybe she was an adventurous soul too?

"I doubt there are pirates or even Indians. Quebec is supposed to be a bustling port for trade."

"But we aren't going to Quebec—well, not directly, that is. This is a village that is supposed to be not far and within a day's travel from there," Elizabeth chimed in, staring out the window. "Besides, I think we should rather wonder if they will expect all of us at once. If I were a man searching for a bride, I would be a little overwhelmed at all of us arriving together."

"What if they are only wanting one of us?" Ella asked, horrified. "I can't go back home. I desperately need this to work out."

"Well, if they only want one of us, you are welcome to whoever put out the ad luring all of us women to town. It reminds me of the story, the Pied Piper, where the rats were lured out of town by a very pretty song. We're the rats, ladies." Rose said impatiently. "And If that's the case, I will just try to find another means of getting a roof over my head for the night."

"The church will put you up," Aurora interjected quietly.

"No. They will assuredly take you in, but it's not my destiny," Arielle denied flatly, wincing.

"I would prefer not to think of myself being a disgusting rat either, Rose. Speaking for all of us, we signed up for adventure and already feel like a heathen running from taking the veil," sighing heavily, Arielle continued on.

"I want love and romance—and I'm just not cut out for a nunnery. My mother was so ashamed of me and ordered me to leave home. I can't go back either, Ella. The church will always take you in, even if you aren't meant for a life of piety."

"We'll be there shortly, so there is no point in worrying now."

"It has been a lovely trip so far, ladies."

"I hope my groom is kind."

"I just hope my suitor has all his teeth and bathes."

"Mercy! What if he snores?"

"Worse... what if he..."

"Enough," Rose laughed, unsure where the conversation was going, but the surrounding women were worrying themselves silly and their imagination was getting the better of them—all of them. She just hoped for a warm home, a kind groom who would tolerate her eccentric behaviors, and possibly be someone that enjoyed the things she did.

She loved to hunt and fish or explore the woods. Occasionally she would tend garden or bake bread, but in truth, she was an awful homemaker and regardless of who she married? She was definitely getting the better end of the deal and probably ought to warn the man before she married him.

As the train pulled to a stop, Rose pulled her shawl around her almost as a protective measure. She was antsy and nervous. Who wouldn't be? They were all about to agree to marry a stranger, sight unseen, in a world she knew nothing about. Hopefully, there were several strangers and not just one lecherous man! If so, she would need to be quick on her feet and come up with another solution fast.

She'd never been this far north, nor seen this part of the country. Bears and other wild animals were a possibility. She'd heard of deep snows in the north, wild Indians, and other challenges, but she was not prepared to venture off alone in a strange land ill-equipped.

She would certainly do so, if she had to!

Stepping off the train, Rose almost lost her footing as she saw the world before her. Grand, sweeping forests created a horizon just above the rooftops of the buildings in the distance. Several greyish streams of smoke pierced the sky, showing where homes were spotted across the breathtaking landscape before her. Moss, grasses, shrubs, and thickets made the vegetation look almost lush and surreal.

It was vibrant.

She saw several people walking about, wagons and horses waiting patiently, as merchants and townsfolk went about their daily business as if nothing was out of the ordinary. She heard languages of every sort being spoken, some English, some French, and another guttural one that she didn't recognize.

Nothing abnormal about this town... except the throng of brides who were disembarking off the train to be paraded before these very people!

"Bonjour? Ou et a sortie?"

"You don't happen to speak any English, do you?"

"Oui, but most speak French here, *compre?* May I help you?"

"Are you the sheriff or magistrate?"

"Yes—and you are...?"

"Very confused? We are apparently waiting on someone to come and meet us so we can meet the person who sent for us. You see, we all responded to a mail-order ad in the paper back home. I am from Boston..."

"I'm from Virginia."

"Maine."

"Pennsylvania."

"Oui, oui...," he said, holding up his hands and smiling. "You've all travelled very far, *non?* You are probably waiting for these then, *eh?"*

He held out several letters. Each paper looked to be folded in thirds and had a wax seal on the seam. It looked very official and regal—except there were no markings on the wax other than a heart pressed deeply in it. It was... charming?

"What's that?" Penelope asked, accepting the billets as she was closest to Arielle. She looked at them and shrugged. They were not addressed to anyone.

"Je ne se pas? You tell me? It arrived on my doorstep this morning with another folded message addressed to me personally."

"I don't understand."

"You women are a blessing to this town and it takes a kind, warm, loving heart and dedication to God's answering our desperate calling."

"What are we doing?" Rose asked skeptically, because now she was truly curious. The man was looking at them like they were the best people ever expected to arrive. You would

6

have thought the crown prince had disembarked the train and was standing before him.

"You are here to marry, yes?"

"Yes, we all answered the ad in the paper."

"Then, you are a blessing to us all."

"Why is that?"

"Because there has been a miasma hanging over this town and we need new life, new chances, brought here. The cholera that took half the population of Lore Valley is gone— but it didn't just kill off our friends and family… it drained the very *joie de' vivre,* leaving nothing but despair. You are our chance at happiness, companionship, and hope."

"I am still confused," one woman whispered. "What is with the letters? There are more of them here than there are women."

"I'm not sure," the sheriff answered. "My letter said to be here today to meet the first set of brides." He turned to look around and hesitated. "A few of us are still arriving."

"What?"

"We received notice yesterday that several mail-order brides would turn up over the next few weeks for the eligible men in town— your grooms- and I assume that is what your letters are too."

"*Assuming*? Who set this all up? I'd like to ask some questions."

"So would we all," he said laughing. "It seems to be a mystery. No one knows who sent the letters, from what I can tell. Everyone has questions, but none of us are about to turn away a chance to marry a lovely kind woman—which you all appear to be."

"Who are you marrying? You have a letter, right?" Belle interjected.

"*Oui,*" he said, tipping it forward from his head in a mock salute.

"Who is your special lady that you are meeting?"

"We," the sheriff said, looking around to the men standing nearby who all held their letters, "all of our papers are blank with only directions to arrive here when the train pulls in."

"No particular lady, eh? Well then I guess you're going to be my guy," Belle said vivaciously, smiling brightly and boldly walking up to the sheriff. "I adore a man of the law and you, sugar, are certainly that. I don't need some crazy letter to tell me my future."

"What about the rest of the billets?" Elizabeth gaped, looking stunned as Belle practically threw her arms around the sheriff, hugging him without a care in the world.

Proper ladies just didn't do that!

A few men rode up on horseback and others walked towards the train depot. Rose was feeling particularly like she was being corralled in by a herd of desperate men. It was a terrible feeling, almost nightmarish! A stifling, choking sensation clawed at her and she was fighting the panic bubbling within her.

Looking up, mentally searching for an escape so she could get away and process all of this, she met the eyes of one of the men on horseback, stunned by the intense glare in his gaze as he looked upon the women, focusing on her.

Rose looked away immediately.

His dark eyes looked so sad, so haunted, and so very bitter to see all the women standing there. Wasn't this their idea to have mail-order brides arrive? He could just leave if he wasn't happy... right? Could she leave? Where would she go?

Arielle hurriedly opened one envelope and looked at the other girls, her eyes wide as she met Rose's. The paper in her hand shook as she suddenly handed the envelopes to each girl. Rose accepted hers numbly as they pressed it in her hand, watching the others as they tore them open.

"What does it say?"

"I think this is who we are presumed to be paired with," Arielle whispered quietly as she looked around. "My paper says a name, someone named Jacques?"

"That's me," a bold voice said out of the crowd.

Rose watched amazed as Arielle's expressive face flushed as she looked at him, her eyes alight with curiosity and surprise.

"You don't have to go with him," Rose hissed, grabbing her arm, only to have Arielle pull away with a smile.

"Rose, he has kind eyes and this chance at a new life is so much better than what I left behind. I need this opportunity. I have nothing and could use a little kindness in my life," Arielle whispered. "I'm willing to take a chance because I have nothing left to lose anymore. I think that is why we are all here, aren't we?"

Rose watched stunned as other women opened their envelopes and slowly got paired up with the men standing before them waiting. She saw several hopeful pairs of male eyes on her as she stood alone on the platform. One man stepped forward to check the train to see if anyone still remained on board, before turning away and walking off.

These people, these men, were literally just waiting for them and truthfully—there wasn't enough women that arrived on this train. She felt almost guilty that in her hands she only held one name. It was a little nerve-wracking and intimidating to think that so many men were just happy at the chance to meet her... regardless of how she acted or what her past was.

Were they so very desperate?

What had created such a demand, a need?

Unfolding her envelope, she stared at the paper before her. The silence was deafening as she stared at the bold name written on the sheet before her. This person was to be her husband if she accepted him.

It was the craziest thing to imagine, and she knew deep down inside it was her choice in the end. She could call out the name and claim a stranger as her own, or she could ignore what could be fate and grasp at a chance with someone else.

Wouldn't she be taking another woman's intended? What if she regretted making her decision and the person's name on the paper was truly kind, picked by chance?

She truly believed deep down inside that everything happened for a reason and she would be rejecting someone who could be a friend—creating hurt feelings and an enemy right away... and she hadn't been in town over five minutes!

"What name do you have?"

"Pardon me?" Rose whispered in surprise, clenching the paper tightly in her fist, almost wadding it up in an effort to hide it. She was nervous, and they were making her even more so. She looked and saw the women she'd arrived with were pairing off like something preordained it.

"We are all waiting for brides to arrive."

"Whose name did you draw?"

"Yes, who?"

Rose swallowed several times, fighting the bubbling anxiety within her as she panicked. They were all watching her, waiting, expecting a miracle from her simply with her arrival, and she knew she was bound to disappoint everyone there—except one.

"Quit dawdling so we can get back to our homes and our lives."

The man on horseback was bold and blunt, causing Rose to look up. She met his eyes once again, and he gave a single nod, not looking away. Was this gesture supposed to give her strength or encouragement? Frankly, his dark shaggy appearance made her a little nervous.

"Wolfe, leave her alone. You don't belong here and you're scaring her."

"I'm not frightened," she bit out immediately as her heart thumped wildly in her chest with dawning comprehension, looking at the man on horseback again and studying him.

"Miss, do you need someone to read it for you?" another man said kindly, stepping forward and reaching for the paper in her hands.

"No," she mumbled, unable to tear her eyes away from the man on horseback. His dark eyes watched her, and she saw him finally look away, his profile strong against the sunlight. He was beautiful in a lonely, broken, wild way... and she realized his name was so fitting, so appropriate.

"I can read it," Rose began. "It says... *Russell Wolfe.*"

"Miss? You don't have to go with him. You can select again."

"What? Why?" she asked, startled.

"It would be better for you; better for everyone."

It was too bad for them that Rose liked a challenge.

She shook her head instead, watching the man in the distance.

Several men's shoulders dropped as they turned away. She fought the urge to say after them *'I'm sorry'* but she had no reason to apologize. Someone had orchestrated this wildly insane matchmaking event and truthfully, she needed a place to get her bearings where she could be left alone.

She didn't want to feel like she'd let people down again, nor did she want to be a part of a happy, energetic village. Disappointing people ate at her soul, leaving scars no one would ever know about. She wanted privacy to lick her wounds, a place to be herself, and could only wish that whoever her potential husband was—that he was kind to her.

Instead, she had just accepted a man that barely acknowledged her. Picking up her single bag, she thrust her chin upwards bravely, accepting fate, an unknown future, and the man before her without looking back. She'd made her choice when she got on the train, and now it was time to pay the mysterious piper.

CHAPTER 2

RUSSELL WOLFE AWOKE EARLIER THAT MORNING, COVERED IN sweat.

Dunking his head in a bucket of water, he shook out his shaggy hair and then rinsed his body, effectively waking him the rest of the way by the cool temperatures. This was becoming a pattern for him, not one that he welcomed either, as he thought of how much his life had changed in the last year.

The nightmares that haunted him seemed to increase in intensity as of late. It was as if he was being driven mad by the rampant idea surging through the town. Someone had mentioned a hairbrained scheme months ago that seemed to have taken root in the minds of the men left picking up the pieces of their lives.

Cholera had wiped out everything. Within a matter of weeks, more than half of the town had died of illness, to where they were being secluded and shunned by other towns nearby. Promised marriages were suddenly broken, trade had stopped, and even the passing priests were avoiding them like the plague.

Lore Valley felt like it was cursed.

He witnessed firsthand as the cholera wiped out both friend and foe, leaving him alone, bitter, and hostile, on the outskirts of this dying town. His lovely bride, Jacqueline, had wept bitter tears as she faded from this world before his very eyes.

They'd only been married a matter of months, but that short time had felt like heaven. Jaqueline was everything he wasn't, a rose among the weeds. She brought happiness with her sweet little laugh, making others seem to want to be near her.

He certainly did.

At first, he was pretty sure she would reject him as so many others did in the past. He'd been called a heathen, an Indian, a pariah, but he couldn't help how he was raised. He was happy to be alive and able to take care of himself now that they were so secluded from the trade ports in nearby Quebec.

Instead, his pretty Jacqueline had smiled, reached out and scratched his beard affectionately, accepting his offer. He'd paid dearly a bride-price for his wife and would have tripled it if they'd asked.

And now she was gone.

The memory of her smile haunted Russell and he heard her laugh at the strangest times, as if she was still there watching out for him. She never saw him for the abandoned boy he once was, trying to survive; instead she treated him like a beloved husband, a man, and her death left him feeling hollow.

He couldn't help but feel angry or bitter at the fact she was gone, nor could he fight the rage at the discovery of the ultimate betrayal from one of his neighbors. Someone had gone behind all of their backs, placing an ad for mail-order brides. He had only discovered this when the mysterious letters had arrived, indicating a train with several women were on the way to meet their new husbands.

It was when his letter appeared under the crack of his front door-that was when the duplicity of this unknown matchmaker hit home. He was one of the widowers of Lore Valley. Someone had made the decision to throw his name into the ring because his Jacqueline had passed away. At first glance, he'd felt a surge of hope at the fact that he wouldn't be so alone anymore, but it was quickly followed by anger and disgust.

What kind of woman travelled to the wilds of Canada to marry a man she didn't know? What kind of man accepted some unknown woman for his own? The answer to both questions was easy: desperation and loneliness.

He heard the train in the distance and knew what that sound meant. The first batch of brides were to arrive shortly. He ultimately thought he would ignore the calling sound of the locomotive, but found his curiosity and stark isolation was too much.

Last night's dream had been horrific, leaving him shaken. The cries, the whimpers, the moaning he heard in his sleep all terrified him to the point that he'd awoken covered in sweat, shaking, and had gotten up, afraid to close his eyes again.

He was certain that it was Jacqueline's ghost haunting him.

He felt like there should have been something more he could have done to keep her in this world. More prayers, more medicine? Should he have sent for a shaman from the tribe that raised him—whom he hadn't seen in years and years? Every thought tore through his mind, eviscerating his soul to where he was nearly broken.

Yet, the train was coming... and he was undeniably curious, like a child toying with something dangerous or forbidden.

In no time, Russell was on his horse entering the tiny village. Several women were standing on the platform near where the train stood puffing faint plumes of smoke into the air. He watched as men unloaded several cars full of supplies, mail, and other goods as they looked upon the women almost adoringly.

Fools, he thought wryly. These women had to be as desperate as the imbecile who'd posted the advertisement in the first place. He almost turned his horse around to head back home... when he saw her.

Bold, intelligent eyes blazed from her face. She had high cheekbones and a firm jaw that told him she was not be one to trifle with. The other women were holding hands, cowering together, bending their heads as they whispered amongst themselves... but not this one.

She met his eyes unwaveringly before looking away. *Why?* She didn't look the type to be cowed down or give up; instead, she looked like she welcomed a challenge.

"Quit dawdling so we can get back to our homes and our lives," Russell snapped out brashly, almost as a dare, causing the woman to look up at him where he sat once again.

No, this wasn't some meek girl at all.

She was a strong one!

A backbone was needed to get through some of the tougher times, not one of the simpering milkmaids surrounding her. This woman would make it through another bout of disease, an attack, or a skirmish... heck, she would probably pick up a rifle and fire off a warning shot against anyone that challenged her.

He nodded once at seeing her straighten taller, her back ramrod straight with indignity at his words.

"Leave her alone, Wolfe. You're scaring her."

"I'm not scared," she bit out immediately, almost staring him down. She was looking at him, as if she was measuring his worth, and it made his skin rankle to be judged by this arrogant slip of a girl.

"Miss, do you need someone to read it for you?" another man said kindly, stepping forward and reaching for the paper in her hands.

"No," she countered, still watching him.

She was actually exquisite in a way that was the complete opposite of his wife, Jacqueline. His wife had been sunlight and a sweet breeze. This woman was dark and mysterious. Her eyes looked like obsidian and her hair was nearly as dark as his. The only difference between them was her fair skin, where he was tanned from laboring in the sun for hours on end.

Thinking about her fair skin made him flush with a pang of guilt. He shouldn't be comparing his wife to a stranger who would marry another man.

"I can read it," she said clearly. "It says... *Russell Wolfe*."

Several men's shoulders dropped as they turned away.

Russell clenched the saddle horn in disbelief to keep himself from falling off. His heart hammered in his chest as his name carried in the silence. She was here for him? He felt a wild panic hit him and nearly bolted at the idea of having another woman in his home once again, except she was already walking towards him... claiming him.

Her strong jaw thrust upwards, almost defiantly, as if she dared him to turn her away before everyone. She had one small bag with her and he saw that her clothing looked nearly threadbare. Wherever she was from, she had been struggling to get by. He would need to get her some warmer things to brave the harsh winters here.

He should leave her there.

Let one of the other men waiting for a bride claim her. He

would be a fool to tackle another wife within a year of losing his Jacqueline. He could simply kick up his heels and ride off, leaving her behind… yet, he didn't.

"Are you Mr. Wolfe?" she said boldly, trying to hide the tremor in her voice. He noticed it though and found her bravado enchanting. This brave chit had more courage in her than some men he knew.

"I am. What's your name?"

"Rose."

"Rose what?"

"Apparently it's to be Rose Wolfe, is it not?" she challenged nervously, and he couldn't help the bark of laughter that escaped him in sheer disbelief. He quickly smothered it and held out his hand, doing his best to glare at this obstinate woman. Instead of taking his hand, she gave him her bag and stared at him pointedly.

"Well?"

"Well, what?"

"Are you not going to assist me up?"

"I tried, and you gave me your things instead."

"Try it once more then, Mr. Wolfe," she ordered, her eyes watching him, and her lips pursed. He fought back a smile and held out his hand, helping her up as she mounted the horse behind him.

CHAPTER 3

Rose wasn't sure how this would all be handled, but she was absolutely regretting getting on the horse behind the mysterious Mr. Wolfe. She was used to riding without a saddle, but riding with a man was completely different.

Her body was pressed against his as they rode, completely alarming her. As she debated jumping down to walk back toward town, in the direction they came from, the path suddenly opened into a small clearing, giving her the chance to eye her new home.

... if she chose to stay!

The house before her wasn't much to look at, but it certainly looked warm - and her hands were chilled.

The large timbers were stacked neatly, forming a simple log home that looked to have seen better days. Weeds were growing up around the building and there wasn't one flower within sight. A small sapling was growing up alongside of the structure, like it was struggling to free itself and the house was stepping on its roots to keep it pinned in place. Cords of wood were heaped sloppily along the side of the house, and she could see a stump in the distance where the rails were split for the fireplace. It was in disrepair and looked like it had been just left to exist, uncared for.

"I saw the priest in town. I'm sure he will marry quite a few people today before heading back towards Levis and Quebec," Russell's voice said suddenly, interrupting the silence as he swung down from the horse.

She expected him to extend a hand towards her and frowned when he didn't. Instead, undaunted, she slid down on her own as he walked towards the house.

"You don't have a priest here in town?"

"Nope," he said simply over his shoulder. "Too small of a town and we have to wait for him to come around for baptisms and..."

Rose noticed her new groom grew awfully quiet, hesitating for a moment, his back stiff towards her.

"We have to wait for everything."

He began walking again, holding her bag, and entered the log cabin structure. The darkness seemed to swallow him up and looked a little intimidating as she stood there in the small glen. Hearing a noise behind her, Rose looked over her shoulder expecting to see it was the horse they'd just dismounted... but instead it was another horse arriving.

"Is Mr. Wolfe inside?" the man said kindly.

"Yes, sir."

"Please, call me Father Demers. I am here to marry you both so you may both live in God's graces," he began before sliding down off his horse. Russell took that moment to reappear, giving an audible groan of frustration.

"You might give me a moment, Father," Russell said tightly. "I'm not even sure this is right for either of us. I was just about to ask Rose if she'd changed her mind after all. I'm sure there would be someone in town better suited to being married."

"Jacqueline never complained about you and was very happy, my son."

"Jacqueline?" Rose chirped, catching the other female's name immediately. Her prospective groom was actually married before, and now a widower? "What happened to your wife?"

"Cholera," the priest said gently. "She was a very pious woman."

Rose watched Russell for several moments and noticed that he didn't say a word, nor did he make any moves in either direction. It was almost like they were in a stalemate.

"Could you give us just a moment, Father Demers?" Rose coughed, trying to act proper. At his nod, she picked up her skirts and walked towards Russell, watching him.

"May we talk candidly?" she whispered in a hushed voice, and saw the look of surprise on his face.

"You were married before and I assume it was for love? This isn't either of our ideal choices, but I need a place to stay and want my freedom. I'm not going to be the best wife you could ever have, but I will stay out of your way."

Russell didn't say a word, just watching her.

"I like it out here, away from prying eyes, and could use someone on my side. If you don't want to marry again, it's okay. We are strangers and there are no hurt feelings. I can ride back into town with the priest, if that is something you'd prefer."

She saw his lip twitch for a moment as he glared at her.

"I know you speak English," she bit out flatly.

"Are you quite finished?" he retorted.

"I'll get my things," she replied, pushing past him, only to have him grab her elbow. She looked at his hand in surprise where it rested, her eyes shooting upwards to meet his.

"I didn't ask for this," he said simply, "... and you aren't very convincing."

"I won't live somewhere unwanted again," she replied honestly. His eyes widened as he frowned deeply before dropping his hand.

"I will not push myself on you, nor do I want to be married to someone who rejects me. I've had enough of that from everyone else around me. I won't have it here too."

"It's the same for me," she whispered in surprise at his muttered words.

"What do you want?" he asked bluntly. "Do you want to ride back into town with the priest—or do you want to stay?"

"What do you prefer?"

He stood there silently, unwavering.

Rose realized that the man before her was giving her a choice. She could choose him, a stranger, who promised not to touch her. She'd already confessed wanting her freedom to do what she wanted, and he hadn't run away or rejected her. Maybe this was her next move, her next path before her...

"I think I'll stay, if you'll have me."

His answer was to extend his arm towards her in response.

Russell was acting like a perfect gentleman, so polite and proper towards her, but donned in garments that looked like they cost no more than her own threadbare dress did. His trousers had seen better days, his rough shirt was functional and had been mended in a place or two, and his jacket was made of leather, whip stitched at the seams by hand.

He looked almost as unkempt and wild as his name—and somehow it seemed to fit.

Rose took his arm, turning back towards the priest, who waited patiently as they stepped forward to say their vows. She accepted on faith that this was the road she was supposed to travel down, praying that she was making the right choices.

Deep down inside, Rose somehow knew that she could

trust Russell. He hadn't been cruel to her… abruptly rude and blunt? Yes… but maybe that was his personality.

Being headstrong, bucking against what was considered normal, and fighting for what felt right in life… well, that seemed to describe both of them. It was as if they each felt the struggle to find themselves and could use someone at their back, on their side, protecting them.

If he could be that person for her, she could certainly have his back and be on his side… as his wife.

Rose listened as he promised to care for her, protect her, and honor her. She noticed he said nothing of love… nor did he ask for her obedience. This caused him to raise yet another notch in her book! She repeated his words, promising her loyalty towards him and vowing to honor him.

They held hands, and she felt hers tremble slightly as a momentary fear took over, and she realized they were now married. Instead of her groom kissing her, he raised her hand to his lips. He politely kissed her knuckles before stepping back and thanking the priest.

She stood there; her arms wrapped around her middle as if she was unsure for the first time at what to do with herself. Did she go towards the house? Was she supposed to stand beside her new husband? As the priest rode off, it revealed her answer to her unspoken question in a dismaying manner.

Russell looked over his shoulder at her.

"Take your time and make yourself at home. Settle in and put away your things, wife. I will be back at dusk."

She watched, dumbstruck, as he walked towards his horse. In a single, smooth, elegant move, he climbed on the animal with practiced ease. He galloped off, leaving her there in the small glen before the log cabin.

What kind of man took off, leaving his new bride alone? she mused.

She felt worse and more rejected than ever before, as she looked around the emptiness surrounding her. Her new husband disappeared from sight into the forest, and only the sounds of the wind through the trees could be heard. The hair on the back of her neck pricked with awareness as she realized she was truly, utterly alone... and disliked it.

A husband that did exactly as you asked, Rose.

WALKING INTO THE HOUSE, Rose looked around and hesitated. For a moment, she wondered if she should have left with the priest as she surveyed the shadows surrounding her. Her husband was a pig, and this was obviously his sty...

The basin was halfway filled with water and several tin plates, still stuck with debris on them, were submerged. The water had a distinct film to it and looked to have been there for a few days. Shivering in disgust, she turned away and looked at the rest of the room.

An enormous fireplace loomed in the darkness, and Rose stumbled on something on the flooring as she headed towards the oil lamp on the mantle. The small single window let in enough light to cast a shadow across the room to keep her from walking blindly inside... but then again, perhaps blindly would have been okay. She lit the oil lamp and looked around, grimacing.

Perhaps she would pick up before she unpacked her things? She might not be the greatest homemaker, nor inclined to do things like cross-stitching or mending, but she preferred to not trip over items scattered across the floor. Setting her bag down on the table, careful not to overturn anything, she sighed.

Rolling up her sleeves, she set herself to work.

First, Rose picked up everything on the floor, refusing to

identify any of it. If it looked like fabric, it went in one pile to be washed. If it vaguely resembled a dish, it went in the now empty sink basin. She had the stove heating so she could boil water in order to wash the filth from the plates and the house in general.

Anything else was swept into a pile, and it went in the refuse bin to be taken out later and tossed into the woods. There were chunks of dried mud, crusts of bread, a cracked globe bottle and a medicinal bottle of bitters that was intact yet empty.

As she made her way throughout the house, she saw that it was only the front of the house that appeared to be lived in. A blanket was strewn over a small cot along the back wall. As she peered around the fireplace, it stunned her to see that there was another chamber before her—a lovely bedroom— that was completely untouched.

A hand carved headboard caught her attention first. Pale wood, with deeply carved pinecones and leaves, practically gleamed against the roughhewn wooden logs that made up the walls. A large quilt was carefully hand-tied with yarn, dotting several simple handmade blocks with color.

Two small seats sat near each other in the corner beside a table that held playing cards. A large dresser was covered with a tatted doily that was grimy with dust and age. The faint feminine air to the room made her realize that this must have been his wife's room, *their room*, before she passed away.

Turning, she looked back out into the kitchen area and saw the cot again as she realized that her new husband couldn't bring himself to be in this room. Tears touched her eyes and she felt a sensation of pity for the man... he must have loved her very much.

No wonder Russell didn't balk at her request to be left alone and promised not to touch her... he couldn't. He still loved his wife. It was an unsettling feeling to look around and see that she was quite literally stepping into someone else's house.

If this was to be her new residence, her home, from now on, she would need to put her own touches on the place. She would never take Russell's memories from him, but if they were to be amicable or become friends... and for Rose to be content living here... there would have to be some semblance of who she was within the home.

She peeled the disgusting doily off the top of the dresser with perverse pleasure as it unstuck itself slowly from the wood with a satisfying sound. Shivering, she gave a nod of approval and walked over to drop it in the laundry pile of clothing. The first thing she planned on doing was making this room habitable—and her own.

Russell could keep his cot, she thought with a grin as she poured the scalding water into the basin to clean everything —starting with the grimy tops of the tables and dresser. She hadn't even opened any of the drawers, knowing they would be full of Jacqueline's things.

Rose had to have a place to put her own items in the home. She wasn't about to unpack her things if just setting them down was going to add to her workload. Rolling up her sleeves, she scrubbed and polished every surface within the cabin.

Having everything clean, tidy, and rearranging it all to suit herself, Rose could find some items to whip together for a light dinner. She made some biscuits, fried ham, and some pickled green beans that she sincerely hoped were just pickled... and not turned within the jar.

Yawning, she looked out the window and saw that it was long past dusk, yet Russell wasn't back yet. Giving up, she dimmed the lamp, setting it on the kitchen table that was made with hewn planks of wood that were sanded until smooth and now no longer sticky. She made her way to the bedroom and collapsed onto the bed, fully dressed and utterly exhausted.

RUSSELL KNEW he was avoiding Rose.

She'd charged into his life, laying claim to him, taking one look at her pretty face, and caving in like a spineless cur. He had been resigned to living a life full of nightmares, rejection, and loneliness after Jacqueline had died... but that was before Rose arrived in town.

The woman with the stubborn streak that had taken his world by storm when she pulled him aside and claimed to be a horrible wife but wanted a where she could be free and be away from others.

Wasn't that just like him?

He'd been turned away so many times for being different, but having been raised by Indians, it taught him to look past the person's appearances and into their heart.

He did just that—and it shook him.

Rose was just like him... but so much more.

Russell didn't want to find her agreeable. He didn't want to feel protective of her when the simple words of past rejections had slipped past the walls of his heart, getting under his skin. He didn't want to relate to her in any way at all-much less feel a kinship with his new bride.

Walking into the house quietly, the smell of soap and the scents of freshly cooked food struck him. A plate was waiting on the table for him, piled high with biscuits that were glossy from melted butter smeared all over the crust. A piece of fried ham, now cold, waited for him. Instinctively, he lifted a foot to step over the debris that had been there near the table for about three weeks, and immediately felt like a fool.

The mess was gone, and he was hovering with his boot just above the floor. Shame filled him as he realized the impression he'd just made on his new bride...

... *Whom was missing?*

Peering around the house, he felt a pit of dread hit him as he realized the only place Rose could be was in Jacqueline's bedroom. Leaning forward, he saw her lying there, softly snoring, on the bed that he and his wife had once shared. Jacqueline never snored... and this was just another difference between the two women.

Hesitating, he realized that there had been several changes around the house that were long overdue. Russell walked back to his cot he'd occupied since before his wife had died and sat down hard next to the folded blanket and fluffed pillow.

He stared at the pillow for several moments, his mind racing. He'd once distanced himself for the comfort of his wife during her illness... and now it was apparent he was doing the same thing again.

There was another difference between his long-dead wife and his new bride: while both were lovely beyond measure and both held a spark of vitality that was enchanting...

Rose was here now.

Jacqueline was in his past.

Getting past the emotions within him that came with that realization would take quite some time to get used to. Not only was he dealing with guilt, a flicker of hope, and embarrassment for how he'd existed before today... now he was wallowing in regret because of a promise he'd made in haste.

He'd sworn not to touch Rose... and would keep his promise.

CHAPTER 4

Rose was feeling decidedly ignored.

She'd asked for freedom and to be left alone... but perhaps this was a bit excessive. They had been married for two weeks and she had yet to see her husband at all. The two of them had fallen into a pattern unwittingly, and she wasn't sure how to reach him.

Each morning, she awoke, and Russell was already gone.

Each evening, she spent it alone and tried to keep busy so she wasn't miserable and didn't cry herself to sleep. She could certainly use some companionship, no matter how abrupt, gruff, or strained it was. She wanted to talk to someone, to laugh or tease them, and she was desperately lonely.

In fact, she waited and waited at the table for him to return, only to fall asleep where she sat. When she awoke this morning, she realized that he'd carried her into the room and placed her on the bed, her wrapper still tied around her waist in a bow. He never bothered her nor touched her... that was even more confusing and frustrating.

She didn't really want some man pawing at her, especially a stranger, but she was married to the confounding man!

What if she wanted children of her own someday? That would require them to be in the same room at some point. Had she run him out of his own home by her request? Was marrying him the greatest mistake of all, dooming her to a life of bitter loneliness?

In fact, out of desperation, she was walking into town today to pick up a few goods. In the past few days, she'd tried tempting him with fresh foods, making some of her favorites from childhood. Fresh bread, scones, a small crumble cake... those items had used up all the flour that she'd found in the makeshift pantry along the wall. She intended to buy some more groceries in an attempt to lure her husband into a conversation or spend five minutes with her.

Gathering up a basket, she made the long trek into town and shivered at the winds blowing off the St. Lawrence river in the distance. It would be a very chilly winter, more than anything she'd ever dealt with back home in Boston—and it got quite frigid there in January.

As she entered town, Rose noticed that several people were watching her curiously, their eyes piercing. A few people ducked their heads together, whispering. Rose clenched her teeth tightly, knowing deep down inside they were discussing her.

"Rose!"

Turning at her name, she saw Ella walking towards her.

"Hello Ella," she said politely with a smile. "You are looking well."

"You are too! Are you alright?"

"Yes, why?"

"I've heard all sorts of things, and the gossip is quite rampant, about your new husband. I hear heathens raised him and no one has seen you for the last two weeks. I was afraid you might be ill or injured."

"People are saying... that?" Rose whispered painfully.

"Yes! Apparently your husband is the town pariah and the only reason he's tolerated is because of his wife who'd passed. She apparently was some saintly creature everyone loved... Oh!"

Ella suddenly grew quiet as Rose winced.

She was certain there was no way she would ever win her husband's friendship at this rate. The town pariah? Everyone disliked him in town?

"Why do they call him... *that*..." Rose asked, choking on the words. He had been curt, abrupt, but unfailingly polite in the rare times she'd talked with him. Russell didn't seem like he was raised by heathens—in fact—he'd acted like a gentleman for the few minutes that she talked to him. Did he know the town viewed him as such? Where did he go then when he left the house? He obviously wasn't coming here!

"I don't want to gossip if it's not true, nor do I want to hurt my friend anymore than I already have," Ella said apologetically. "I'm so relieved to see you and glad you are okay."

"I'm more than fine," Rose lied baldly. "I'm thrilled and Russell is off working today."

"I heard he is the chief supplier of furs here. You must be really proud and doing quite well for yourself," Ella beamed, linking her arm with Rose's. "I've got to get some items from the mercantile. Are you headed there too?"

The chief supplier of furs?—But he was the town pariah? That made no sense!

"Yes," Rose said distractedly, the words spinning in her head. "I have been making Russell many treats to eat. I am quite happy," she repeated, wishing it was true.

Walking into the mercantile, they abruptly stopped Rose.

"We don't serve your kind here, Injun-lover," the man said bluntly, spitting a stream of tobacco juice onto the floor. Waves of embarrassment rolled over Rose as she froze instantly, praying the clerk wasn't talking to her.

"I beg your pardon?"

"Oh Rose," Ella's voice said beside her, full of pity and remorse. "We'll just go or I can get what you need, honey."

"You heard me! Now get out. We don't cater to your kind."

"There must be some mistake," Ella asked.

"You married to that varmint Russell Wolfe?"

"Yes."

"Then you aren't welcome in my shop. We don't cater to your kind here in my store. Now, get!"

"I need nothing from that man," Rose said tautly, fueled by shame at how brutally she was treated and how her husband was depicted in town. Whatever was in his past obviously would affect her, and this was the first instance of it.

Frustrated beyond belief and mortified, Rose bid her friend a quick goodbye and practically raced out of town as quickly as possible before the tears started falling. This had been a mistake!

The worst one yet...

She'd gone from rejected by others back home to ostracized for nothing... and her heart was breaking! Scalding hot tears streaked down her face as she sobbed wildly, walking down the path carrying her empty basket.

What was she supposed to do? Did this mean that she couldn't talk with anyone in town for fear that they would all treat her like this? What did he mean by calling her those names?

They received her husband in town, but only barely so, because of his prior marriage to Jacqueline... but how could she compete with a saintly ghost of a woman? He was avoiding her. She was lonely, and had no chance at all at finding her place, here in her new home.

Everything around her seemed to go from bad to worse!

RUSSELL WAS SKINNING a rabbit in the woods when he heard sobbing. Deep, gut-wrenching, sobbing. Getting to his feet, he tossed the knife into the grass and quickly washed his hands in a creek nearby, wincing at the cool waters against his warm skin. As he peered through the trees, he saw Rose wiping her eyes angrily as she practically marched down the lane.

Why was she crying?

"Rose!" he blurted out, emerging from the woods unthinking, wincing as he realized that she might not want to be seen crying, nor would she want to be bothered by him. "Rose? Are you alright? Did you hurt yourself?"

Surprised, he held back a grin as she threw the basket on the ground angrily, rounding on him. Russell crossed his arms against his chest, almost relieved that the spark of fire within her was still there. He could handle anger, but tears always unmanned him.

He was a sucker for tears.

"I abhor the clerk at the mercantile," she seethed, clenching her jaw tightly and inwardly fuming. "I know I'm not supposed to hate, that it's not the Christian thing to do, but there is a special place for bitter people that get enjoyment from humiliating people..."

"What?" Russell interrupted, unwinding his arms as he stepped towards her. "What happened? Is that why you are crying?"

"He was particularly hateful towards us, calling me a terribly uncouth name."

"What did he say?" he asked, turning her chin towards

him so she would look at him. He saw the anger and hurt deep within her dark eyes.

He knew that feeling, and it wasn't a good one. He'd felt it several times in his life and wanted to save his new bride from ever having to deal with that humiliation.

"I don't want to repeat it."

"He called you this name in front of others?" he said quietly, trying to keep the anger from his voice. It was one thing for that slovenly man to take his money and treat him like garbage—but he would never allow his wife to ever be dealt with like that.

"Yes," Rose mumbled, looking away from him. He saw her cheeks turn bright red and knew she was really bothered by whatever had happened. A single fat tear slid down her cheek and landed on his thumb, making his heart clench painfully.

"What did you need from the store?"

"Nothing," Rose replied, stepping backwards away from him, her tone bitter and full of pain. "I don't need a thing from anyone."

He watched her walk back towards the log cabin, alone. Turning towards the town, he walked with a purpose. No one would ever make his wife cry! He could handle the rejection since he'd dealt with it all his life, but Rose was innocent of his past and his heritage.

Hours later, Rose stirred the pot of stew on the stove when a knock at the door was heard. It was just enough to send her on another round of crying, if that was Russell knocking on his own front door. Her poor wounded nerves couldn't handle much more, and she felt very close to her breaking point.

Yanking open the door, she almost slammed it but hesitated at the alarmed look on the clerk's face as he stood there nervously looking around.

"What do you want?" she said bluntly.

"I've come to apologize, M-Mrs. Wolfe," he stammered, again looking off to his side. Rose quickly stepped forward out from the doorway and surveyed the glen around the house.

"What are you looking for?"

"Nothing!"

"Then why are you sweating?"

"Because I came to say that I'm sorry and to bring you a few things," he blurted out. "I won't ever be rude to you again and you can consider them a gift."

"I want you off my property—*that* is the only gift you can give me."

"NO!" he blurted out loudly, wincing, before repeating it quietly.

"No, please. I want to make it up to you and feel really bad about what happened. I truly am sorry and I need to make this right."

"Why?" Rose said, squinting her eyes at the man. "Why do you need to make this right? I don't understand this sudden change and frantic urge to be nice to me. You made your intentions quite clear this afternoon how you felt doing business with my husband and I."

"And I regret it! Wholeheartedly!"

"Where is my husband?" she asked baldly, knowing he had something to do with this and feeling slightly pleased that he stood up for her. She didn't know what he'd said, but it was enough to make this bully quake in his shoes.

"Oh, gracious…" the clerk breathed, paling. "Please don't call for him. Let me just get your things and I'll leave."

"I won't take them unless you let me pay. We don't need your charity and won't be beholden to you," she retorted.

"I won't take payment."

"Then it will not be accepted. The last thing I want is for you to have anything at all negative to say about the Wolfes. We won't owe you anything."

"Please!" he squawked nervously, patting his forehead with a handkerchief. "Please, just take it and tell your husband everything is forgiven once again. My outburst will never happen again, I swear it."

"You had better not treat ANYONE like that ever again or I will send Russell back in your direction. Are we clear?" Rose said grimly, trying desperately to keep the smile from her face. Whatever Russell had done to the man had to have been something!

Stunned, she watched the clerk from the mercantile begin to unload things from his wagon right there in the yard. A large bag that looked like a feed sack landed with an oomph. He set several small brown bags with folded tops on it. A bolt of material appeared in the pile and Rose immediately stopped him.

"What are you doing? I only came to your store for flour."

"Flour? How much flour? I only brought a small bag…"

"What is all of this then?"

"Goods."

"I can't take all of this," she sputtered inelegantly. "I only have a few dollars on me and didn't plan on spending that much today."

"It's on sale then," he said quickly, putting the rest of it down. "I'll be on my way now. Tell your husband everything is fine between us and I promise it will never happen again. You are welcome at any time."

"I will—but I want you to tell others that too."

"Of course, Mrs. Wolfe."

The man hopped into the wagon awkwardly and quickly left.

Stunned, Rose realized she was still holding the three dollars she had on her person from this morning when she had gone into town. She really didn't relish the thought of having to go back and pay him—but she also wouldn't accept it for free from him.

Walking over, she picked up one of the small brown sacks and opened it. He'd brought her brown sugar! Kneeling down, she peered inside the other bags and saw coffee, rice, flour, and powdered sugar. The large bag was full of grain and the bolt of fabric was a soft rich calico that felt so smooth under her hand.

This was too much!

Getting to her feet, she looked around.

"Russell? Are you here? Can you help me carry this?"

Rose almost didn't expect him to be close by since today was the first time she'd seen him truly since they'd said their vows. His unexpected appearance had stunned her when she was walking home earlier in the day... and again now, as he suddenly emerged from the woods.

"What did you say to him?" she questioned him immediately.

"Let's get these things inside," he countered.

"Will you stay for dinner or are you leaving again?" she retorted immediately before softening her tone. She didn't want to ruin the first chance at having another person around to talk to by running him off. If she had to make the first gesture, so be it.

"I'm tired of being alone all the time and I want to talk about what just happened... *please.*"

Just when she thought for a moment that Russell might actually leave, he instead picked up the massive bag of feed along with the bolt of fabric, hefting it onto his shoulders.

Without a word, Rose picked up the other packages and quickly followed behind him.

As they entered the cabin, she felt herself flush with pride as the stew she'd started smelled fragrantly rich and decadent. She'd browned the pieces of meat in butter after letting them soak in a bit of vinegar, breaking down the meat so it was tender and falling apart. She might not be the best wife out there, but this hungry girl *could* cook!

"I'm sorry I don't have any bread for the stew..." she explained in the silence. "That is why I went to town—to get some more flour so you could have some rolls or a loaf of bread to sop up the gravy from your meal."

"It smells delicious," he replied after a moment, setting down the bag of feed by the door. "Where do you want the fabric?"

"If you can set it on the bed, I'll serve up the stew. I don't want to get anything on the material."

The strained awkwardness between them was unsettling.

Rose felt concerned that she might have already ruined her chance of communicating with the one person she should develop a bond with... it certainly wasn't the many townsfolk she'd seen after today's incident. She was leery of them and their quick opinions.

Ella had been the only one to approach her in town like a friend... and that was because they'd bonded quickly on the train ride up towards Lore Valley. A genuine friend told you the good/bad/and the ugly of life without sugarcoating it or softening the blow. She was as good, sweet, honest, and decent as the day was long.

That was Ella.

Lost in thought, Rose quickly filled two stoneware bowls and set them on the table opposite of each other. It wasn't until she noticed Russell standing there, watching her, that she hesitated.

"You are eating… aren't you?"

"You don't mind my company?"

"Truthfully," she began with a sad smile, "I'm really grateful you are here and I've been dying for someone to talk to besides myself. It gets awfully lonely out here by myself."

"I didn't want to bother you."

"There's a difference between bothering me and abandoning me."

"I would abandon no one."

"Then where have you been?"

"Working," he said simply, as if that answered all the problems in the world. Rose fought the urge to roll her eyes and instead took her seat opposite of his place setting. She looked at him expectantly.

"Are you hungry?"

"Yes."

"Then sit down and let's eat."

"I can come back later."

"It will be cold."

"It's okay."

"Why don't you want to sit with me?" Rose said bluntly, watching him as he looked away. "I asked for your company, invited you to join me, and yet you still offer to come back later. Are you waiting for me to be asleep so we can avoid talking?"

"You don't mince words, do you?"

"It's a tragic flaw of mine," she admitted with a slight smile, pointing at the other seat. "Please, sit down and I'll try to be on my best behavior, Russell."

He hesitated for a moment before coming to join her silently at the table. She watched him as he moved, realizing that her new husband was an enormous man and she'd never noticed in the few times she'd seen him. Once was on horseback and the second time was as they'd said their vows. Tall, broad shoulders, and with a dark complexion, she almost dropped her spoon as she understood now why the bigoted clerk had called her names.

Her husband was part Indian.

His dark hair, deep brown eyes, and tanned skin were present, but there was also a little something else there mixed in with his blood. He had a very angular face with a scruffy shadow of a beard on his chin. The more she studied him, the more she realized she was truly seeing him for the first time.

Russell was gorgeous in a wild and untamed way.

His spoon clattered into the bowl as he suddenly stood up.

"You are staring," he said hotly. "I can leave."

Rose gaped and surged to her feet, nearly upending her bowl that was perched on the table. She barely caught it at the same time that her husband's hands reached for the bowl, steadying it. Their fingers touched, and he jerked backwards as if scalded.

"It's hot," she explained quickly. "Are you burnt?"

"No. I'll come back later."

"I'm sorry I was staring at you. I know it's rude...," she began, only to see him walk out the doorway into the evening air without another word. The door closed behind him.

"... But that is rude too," she whispered to the closed door, her eyes brimming with tears of rejection. Uncertain how to reach him and feeling even more alone than ever before, Rose sat down numbly, her mind racing.

Everything within her was screaming out silently that this was a lost cause, another mistake, and she just needed to give up on finding a place she belonged and the happiness she craved.

There was only one problem...

Rose was no quitter.

Russell practically ran from the cabin, his heart pounding.

The tender expression that he saw on Rose's face was his undoing, making him feel things that he never expected or anticipated. He'd stepped forward when she'd called out for his help, carrying in the goods he'd picked out for his new bride earlier in the day when he paid a visit to the mercantile to straighten out a few problems.

Samuel had always been the town gossip, fostering snide remarks tossed his direction. He believed it was because Jacqueline had turned down Samuel's proposal and accepted his own. The bride-price he'd paid her family had been substantial before they'd left their only daughter there, leaving for Ontario... cementing a rift between the two men.

When he stormed into the mercantile, Russell was pretty certain he was going to be shot or hung for his actions, but carelessly he let his rage take over. No one was ever going to make his new bride cry! She was his wife now and treated him well. Russell owed it to Rose to ensure that she received the same courtesy from him.

Grabbing Samuel by the collar, he dragged the fat arrogant clerk over the counter bodily and pulled him into the street before the town. Several men ran forward, but the look on Russell's face made them stop in their advancement towards them.

"You will never address my wife like that ever again!" Russell began loudly so everyone could see and hear him. He wanted the people to know that this wasn't for him, but for Rose. If his wife was treated badly, then perhaps other people's wives were too.

"If you ever shame her, degrade her publicly, or treat other women so disgracefully... I will take the pelts and goods you are so fond of selling up the river to be sold in the next village. Are we clear? I will not do business with a man that verbally abuses my wife."

Russell leaned in menacingly and whispered.

"And if you ever make Rose cry again, these people will find your naked hide staked in the middle of town, skinned like a rabbit."

He released the man angrily, watching Samuel fall in the dirt. As he looked up at him angrily from where he lay, Russell pointed at Samuel's pants with a tight, secretive smile.

"I'll begin right there, Sam..."

Samuel paled, his face turning almost grey.

Russell realized he might have crossed a line, that the entire town was witnessing. He'd let his temper get the better of him, and this was not how he intended to make his mark. He wanted Rose treated with respect and dignity, not ashamed to be married to him.

He extended his hand toward Samuel.

"Now, I would like to purchase the goods you refused to sell my wife—and I believe you should deliver them to her with a heartfelt and sincere apology. Does that sound agreeable?"

Time seemed to tick by as neither man moved. Russell stood there with his hand outstretched in peace, while Samuel looked at him warily. Finally, one of his neighbors, Jacques, cleared his throat noisily.

"That is more than generous of you, Wolfe. I would suggest you take his offer, Samuel, as winter is coming and you'll be needing those fur pelts to sell—won't you?"

"Wolfe is being nicer to you than I would be if you treated my wife poorly," another man said baldly, glaring at Samuel.

"I can't say that I would be as understanding, nor would I continue to do business with someone like that."

Samuel slapped his hand in Russell's and got up off the ground. Russell leaned and whispered in his ear. "Make no mistake, this is for my wife's sake. I would just rather skin your hide now, so you better make your apology to Rose a superb one—got it?"

It was then, in that very moment, that Russell knew he would do anything to make sure Rose was happy marrying him. There was something about her that drew him, and he watched her often from a distance, but tonight was different.

It felt personal... almost surreal.

The longing in Rose's eyes, as she looked at him over the table, shook him to the core. He never saw that look on Jacqueline's face. Oh, Jacqueline had been friendly and sweet towards him, but there was never that open and raw look of attraction between them.

Rose looked at him and saw the man he was—and it made him want to climb over the table and take her in his arms. The surge of longing that exploded within him was overwhelming. He found himself looking at her lips, imagining what they would feel like touching his, and he couldn't breathe.

He needed fresh air... and time to think!

The log cabin had always been his house for the last several years, but tonight, for the first time, it felt like a *home*. He felt pampered, taken care of, and wanted...

Russell didn't feel like he deserved any of that!

CHAPTER 5

THE NEXT FEW DAYS OF SILENCE WERE FILLED WITH THOUGHTS, plans, and schemes that would have made any military general run for fear of his life. Rose may be no quitter, but she was definitely forming a plan of attack. The prize was unlike any other and infinitely precious... to earn the friendship and camaraderie of her estranged new bridegroom.

First, she had to determine just what she Russell was fleeing from. Was it his past? Her past? Her cooking? Did he regret marrying her? Was he still in love with his deceased wife? How can she compete with a ghost of a woman?

Second, Rose needed to figure out exactly what she wanted from him. She told herself repeatedly that she just wanted someone to talk to, but she was forever picturing his face when she closed her eyes. Looking at him the other night over the table made her realize that she was completely and utterly attracted to her husband.

Rose never pictured herself as the type to fawn over a man, nor was she some vapid female who swooned with desire at the sight of a pretty smile... but there was certainly something there that ignited her soul on fire. She imagined what it would be like to see him smile or hear him laugh, yearning for a genuine relationship with her husband.

She wanted it all. His affection, his heart, a bond... the whole fairytale! Now, it was deciding how to get there...

It was another few days before she settled on a plan. And while it was quite out of the ordinary, downright foolish, and a little crazy... there was an off-chance that it might just work!

She decided to woo her husband.

Her plans began by drawing him out into the open.

He appeared quickly when she was walking back from town and had been crying. He also emerged when that nasty clerk had delivered the dry goods, dumping them in the yard. Russell had helped her carry them inside when she asked. So, if she combined the two... that meant she needed to be crying within sight of her husband, and helpless to the point that she had to be cared for.

Using tried-and-true, feminine wiles, she mused ruefully.

Now, once she enacted her plan and got him close, she had to snare him. If she played her hand too soon—he would bolt. She had to be patient, hope he didn't notice the lie, and keep up the pretense so she could get to know him a little better.

Should she feign illness? A fainting spell? Struck down by some mysterious or unknown ague?

Wincing, she remembered that his previous wife died from cholera. That would be downright cold-blooded to pretend to be sick in order to get to know him better... and if he discovered she was lying? She would never regain his trust.

Perhaps something simple, like a sprained ankle?

Clasping her hands together, her breath caught in her chest as a rush of joy hit her. A turned ankle would be just the thing! Russell would find her on the ground, helpless, and possibly crying if she could summon up the fake tears. He could carry his damsel-in-distress back home and nurse her back to health.

It was a perfectly good and solid plan.

What could go wrong?

ROSE AWOKE EARLY the next morning hoping to catch Russell before he left, only to spring out of bed as the door shut softly. Cursing, she peered around the fireplace to see that he had left already. Taking her time getting dressed, she replayed the idea in her head, trying to think of any possible thing that could go wrong.

Smoothing her dress over her form, she glanced at her reflection in the small mirror above the dresser and wash basin, pinching her cheeks for color. She'd plaited her hair before bed, now unwinding it and smiling as she began shaking out the rivulets and curls.

Wrapping a shawl about her shoulders, she began strolling easily, as if she hadn't a care in the world. The biggest problem was that she was beginning to care… a lot.

As she walked, she decided to make an event out of the day, enjoying the sunshine and cool breeze before the weather turned. There was already a sharp nip in the air, causing her to hug her shawl a little closer in an effort to stay warm. The leaves were curling at the edges and turning deep russet colors. It would not be long before fall abruptly turned to winter and the first snows fell.

Each step took her farther in a different direction. She knew what the other way was. That path would soon lead into town or other people travelling toward the village.

That simply would not do.

She needed to be alone and dependent on Russell for this

to work. If she faked a sprained ankle and someone else came upon her, then there would be no heroic rescue in her near future. Sighing happily, she closed her eyes for a moment and took a deep breath, wondering if he was watching her from the forest like before or how long she would have to wait.

WHAT IS SHE DOING?

Russell wondered idly, watching from where he was crouched down in the bushes. He'd been checking his snares and making his way through the trails he knew like the back of his hand, when he saw Rose emerge from the cabin.

She was lovely beyond measure, and he felt guilty for even thinking that.

Russell should still mourn his wife—and a part of him did and always would. He knew deep down he would always miss how accepting Jacqueline was of him, but a bigger part of him recognized the loss of her companionship overall. They didn't have a grand passion that they shared; it was a kindness and affection that was sweet and heartwarming.

Looking at Rose, he knew it wasn't the same.

His heart stuttered in his chest and he longed to hold her hand in his again, just to feel her smooth skin and that tenuous bond. He quite often thought of how they'd held hands as they repeated their vows… just before he ran away.

He saw her collapse in the grass and nearly leapt from his spot, only to see Rose stand up again angrily, stomping one foot. She looked around, her face frowning and decidedly peeved, before promptly collapsing again. On the third time, she sat up and he could hear her muttering something from where he waited, as she fanned out her skirt in the grass before standing up once again… and dropping into the grass, this time laying the back of her hand on her forehead.

Whatever was she doing?

He watched as she walked about the grass, clasped her hands together, and proceeded to collapse onto the ground awkwardly... as if she was trying to make it look pretty—and failing miserably.

This time, she stood up and cursed aloud, before trying again.

Russell held back a choked snort, covering his mouth to keep from revealing himself as he watched, fascinated. The words she'd just uttered aloud would make the most uncouth man blush fiercely, and it was downright laughable.

Rose was actually practicing fainting—and he had no idea why!

She dropped to the ground in several unique positions, sometimes slowly, and other times quite abruptly with an audible *'thud'*. Once she got up, wincing and rubbing her backside indelicately.

Inspecting her skirt, she picked up the hem to inspect a large grass stain, but not before he got a glimpse of her petticoat underneath. She honestly thought she was alone or she would have been scandalized to think that he was viewing the rehearsed drama before him.

Whatever this farce was, he was inclined to play along out of sheer curiosity. Getting to his feet, he emerged from the shadow of the trees.

THIS WAS NOT WORKING *in the slightest!*

Rose was getting downright frustrated because she'd been walking for nearly a half hour with no signs of Russell anywhere. There was no one in the area! It occurred to her that if she was to pretend to sprain her ankle; the event needed to look real or she would be caught in a lie. She dropped to the ground dramatically, and it just felt... wrong.

Trying again, she laid the back of her hand on her forehead... and that wasn't right either.

She wasn't supposed to faint, and that is what other women did when they were having a '*fit of the vapors*'. No, she was supposed to have twisted her ankle, forcing her estranged husband to attend to her.

Plopping down indelicately, she landed directly on a rock with her backside. Wincing and cursing vehemently, she rubbed the spot before looking carefully in the surrounding grass. If she did this when she knew he was watching, she would need to make sure she landed softly or else she might actually get injured.

She tried three more times and was getting worn out. It was a genuine struggle to get off the ground in a corset... and now she had a massive stain on her nicest dress.

Maybe it was just time to give up and go back? She thought, looking up to see Russell emerging from the woods. His face was immobile and passive. He did not look happy to see her... and Rose wondered how long he'd been there.

"I've turned my ankle," she said baldly, curious to see his reaction and if he would say anything about her falling to the ground repeatedly.

"You're... injured?"

At his hesitation and startled expression, Rose knew he'd seen her practicing. It was time to hide her actions, because she hated the idea of him knowing that she lied to get his attention.

Just my pride, she thought, and plastered a pained look on her face.

"Oh, it is aching painfully... in fact, when I put pressure on it – I quite fall to the ground because it will not support me," she announced, trying to keep the pride from her voice as she conjured up the elaborate fable.

Brilliant! You are a genius! Keep going, Rose!

"What are you doing out here? You've walked quite a distance, ending up stranded and alone."

"I'm not alone," she interjected quickly. "You are here now."

"How... fortunate," he replied slowly, watching her.

Uh-oh...

"What are *you* doing out here?" she countered, turning the tables on him. *That's right-throw him off the scent!*

Russell stood there, about ten feet from her, observing her.

He looked almost wild today with his hair pulled back and tied with a queue, giving him an almost rugged appeal. He was so blasted handsome in the faded shirt that was open at the collar. She noticed he had a belt around his hips with two large knives tucked in scabbards, along with a pistol. A rifle was swung onto his back, held by a strap that bisected his chest, accentuating his broad shoulders.

Why on earth did she end up with the most infuriating, stubborn, and gorgeous man in town?

"I'm hunting," he replied flatly.

Me too! She thought wildly and almost laughed.

"You're smiling... so it must not hurt quite so much."

Curses!

She was bungling this!

Rose needed to be quicker on the uptake, cannier with her words, expression, and actions. Being a practiced liar wasn't as easy as it seemed or appeared. She'd never been one for telling fibs in the past because you always ended up caught.

"Only because you're here and I'm not alone anymore. Can you help me get back home?" she beseeched prettily, hoping he fell for it. "I'm not sure how long I can walk on my own—or if I even can."

She looked downwards, hoping it appeared meek to him, and nearly breathed a sigh of relief as he drew closer. He extended his arm towards her, and she tried not to frown.

So much for a lady being swept off her feet by the odious Prince Charming before her...

"Ow," she yelped, taking a step, and pulling on his arm.

"It's that bad?"

"It hurts terribly."

"Maybe I should fetch the horse or perhaps a wagon for you?"

"No, I think I'll make it," she confessed with an exaggerated sigh.

Rose noticed that he looked away, and she wondered if he was angry because she'd interrupted his day. Mortified, she saw him wipe his hand down his face as he looked upwards at the sky before turning back to her. Yes, he was not pleased in the slightest.

"I'm so sorry about this, Russell," she began. "Certainly. I will be right as rain when I rest for a bit. I just need to get home."

"To get that boot off before your ankle swells?"

"Exactly."

"So, we don't have to cut it off of you?" he prompted.

"*WHAT?* My ankle?"

"The boot," he explained, "so we don't have to cut off the boot."

"Oh..." she said, smiling and a little concerned at how this was going. There was absolutely nothing romantic or engaging about this scenario. How was she supposed to build a rapport with the blasted man if he was obviously this thick and obtuse?

"Do you think maybe... you could... help me?"

"That's exactly what I'm doing," he retorted.

"I mean… possibly… um…"

Curses! Was the ogre actually going to make her ask for it?

"Could you perhaps carry me home, so I don't have to walk on it?" she asked, batting her eyelashes like she'd seen some of the other girls do towards their prospective suitors.

"Carry… you?"

"Yes. I think that is a splendid idea and will keep me from injuring my ankle even more."

"You want me to *carry* you?" he repeated, staring at her.

His eyes looked pained, as if he was holding back. Was the idea of carrying her so disturbing to him? Couldn't he see that she needed his help and was reaching out to him? She wanted to appeal to his male pride and hoped that rescuing a damsel-in-distress would make him look at her differently.

Obviously not.

"Yes, Russell. Could you please carry me home so I can rest?" she asked again, every so sweetly, and trying to be encouraging. He was making her want to stomp her foot in frustration—but that couldn't happen or she would be found out for sure!

She knew if she could just reach him, somehow break through that shell, they could begin to be friends and perhaps develop into something more…

"Certainly."

She almost clapped in relief… only to be picked up and swung onto his shoulder like he hefted that sack of feed from the glen the other evening. Her face butted into the rifle, knocking her painfully right in the lip, making impact with her front teeth jarringly.

"Oomph!"

"I'll have you home in no time," he said chokingly, making Rose feel even more discomforted as the blood rushed to her head from her precarious position, flooding her cheeks.

She was mortified.

This was not what she'd intended, nor did she want to hear how he was struggling to carry her weight, like she was too heavy for him. His voice, their tone, and clipped words... everything indicated that he was having a very hard time holding her onto his shoulder.

She'd wanted to be carried off into the sunset... and well, this was a valuable lesson she'd never intended to learn.

Technically, that very event she'd yearned for was happening right now—just not like Rose had pictured it in her mind. She needed to be careful what she wished for... because she was getting a heaping dose of it.

THANKFULLY, the walk back to the cabin was blessedly silent. Rose didn't even hesitate when he put her down at the stoop. Instead, she avoided meeting his eyes and marched right inside, completely forgetting about her supposedly injured ankle... and the wretched cad called her out on it!

"I see you're much better..." he drawled out.

Angrily, Rose slammed the door only seconds before a temperamental shriek unwittingly escaped her. *That confounded man!* He was toying with her and simply didn't care if she was hurt or not.

Instead of checking on her, opening the door and apologizing for teasing her, or trying to make amends with his new bride... the infernal ogre was laughing outside, his voice carrying as he walked away.

Maybe she needed to rethink her plans and whether she wanted to try building a relationship with someone as infuriating as Russell Wolfe was!

CHAPTER 6

Vengeance was a dish best served cold...

Russell realized this to the truest sense of the word that very night as he returned to the cabin to rest. Whatever the reasoning behind his bride's thoughts at having him carry her home, it must have been important to Rose.

He had obviously angered his new bride to a degree he'd never expected or anticipated.

She'd been so sweet, so caring, leaving a meal out on a plate normally for him each night. His dinner was always left warming on the stove, but tonight was different. He could smell that Rose had fried bacon earlier and he could smell the aroma in the air... but that was not what was on his plate that waited for him.

Instead, it was much more obvious that he'd made her quite upset and he would need to mend the rift between them or suffer the consequences... and they were dire!

His plate was on the table waiting for him, only it held a piece of raw salt pork along with two cracked raw eggs.

His temperamental bride was obviously not inclined to attempt to take care of him this evening in retaliation for the affront. She was trying to get him to carry her home, and he'd spent all afternoon laughing repeatedly at how angry she'd been when he set her down.

He'd seen her split lip and instantly felt guilty—but the flames raging in her eyes had made him hesitate for a fatal moment, dividing the two of them like a massive canyon that split the land wide when the door was slammed in his face.

The line was drawn—and it would be up to him to mend the unknown problem.

Why had she wanted to be carried?

That was the most confounding part!

He'd picked her up and carried her, but she seemed to be even more angry that he'd done so. Had he carried her wrong? There were only a few ways to carry a person, and some of them were difficult too…

He had been resetting a snare on the ground when it dawned on him.

His wife had wanted to be held.

Rose had wanted him to carry her against him, in his arms, and he'd missed all the signs. That was why she'd been practicing falling in the grass and mimicking passing out. She thought to trick him into holding her… but why couldn't she just ask?

It wasn't like he would turn away the chance… That, in itself, was a sobering thought, because Russell realized that he'd done that very thing.

He'd turned away from his new wife several times already.

He avoided her and had been trying to give her space to grow accustomed to her new home, but maybe she didn't want that? He'd been trying to settle his mind to the idea of having a different person in his home, in his bed.

It rankled him at first, the idea of Rose sleeping in the bed he'd shared with Jacqueline… but then the soft snores he heard from the other room made him realize that they were two completely different people.

There was so much that had changed over the last few weeks that he was coming to terms with the idea that they could grow into a couple someday... but what if Rose wanted that someday to be much sooner than he did?

Perhaps he was the one digging in his heels and drawing things out?

If his new wife wanted attention, he would go about it the proper way. He would court her, giving them time to get to know each other, and develop a friendship between them. That would give him the much-needed time to settle the chaos in his own mind and in his soul at losing Jacqueline.

Change was hard... even if it ended up being for the greater good—and good things came to those who waited.

He would be very patient and not rush things.

ROSE STARTED at a knock on the front door.

She assumed it was Russell, rolling her eyes as she shoved a lock of her hair out of her face. Figures he would show up during the day when she was trying to plot her next move.

She'd been making bread and rolls all morning long, intending to secret them away until they talked... hopefully before they went stale. She knew the scent of the yeast would hang in the air for a while, and the man obviously loved his bread. Normally she set out two or three rolls with his plate and he never left a scrap or morsel of food behind.

Plus, she felt extremely guilty about leaving him the raw meal last night.

What kind of wife did that to her husband—even during an argument?

It was her duty and obligation to care for him according

to her marriage vows. She'd married him and he didn't have to accept her. He'd taken her under his wing, in his home, and she'd slammed the door in his face. Oh yes, not only did she want to talk... she wanted to apologize.

Opening the door, it stunned her to see Daisy standing there with a wide smile across her lovely face.

"Good morning, sweet friend!" she announced cheerfully.

Daisy was infectiously bright and charming. Her smile always seemed to light up a room, and she'd bonded with the woman, all the women, on the train almost immediately. Rose could have sworn that the woman didn't have an enemy in the world... and if she did? Daisy could charm them out of the momentary lapse straightaway!

It was as if the sun shone a little brighter with her just being there.

"Hello. What are you doing here?"

"I thought I would make the rounds and get out for a bit. I miss seeing everyone and wanted to say hello. Something smells absolutely wonderful," Daisy said brightly. "Are you making bread? I'm delightfully horrid at it and my loaves end up looking like earthen bricks. May I watch you?"

"I doubt anything you do is *'horrid'*..." Rose replied with exaggeration, opening the door a little wider. "Come on inside and I'll make some coffee for us. Would you like a cup?"

"I would adore one."

Letting Daisy inside the cabin, her friend's eyes dropped immediately to the plate on the counter – a single eyebrow raised in question.

Rose winced as she saw Daisy looked at the plate questioningly. She hadn't tossed the raw eggs and salt pork yet, leaving it as a constant visual reminder so she didn't talk herself out of apologizing to Russell.

"You let the eggs come to room temperature like that?"

"No," Rose said immediately. "That was a… mistake."

"I see."

"How are things with you and your new groom? I'm sure he is quite head-over-heels in love with you already," Rose said, changing the subject and trying to keep the bitterness out of her voice.

"I wish…" Daisy sighed, taking a seat at the table and putting her head to rest on her fist inelegantly. "I wish things were going as well for me as they must be for you."

"What in the world are you talking about?"

"Things are strained for us right now," Daisy admitted before perking up and plastering a false smile on her face that didn't reach her eyes. "I am not here to talk about me and my concerns. Let's talk about you and your handsome beau…"

"There isn't much to say," Rose replied, kneading the bread and punching it down. She took a knife and cut the dough in half, putting part of it into a greased earthenware bowl and covering it with a cloth. Placing it on the oven, she shook her head at Daisy.

"In truth, there isn't anything to say other than I might be in over my head."

"In love?"

"No—as in drowning, floundering, very much in trouble…"

"Why do you say that?"

"Because we haven't said nary a thing to each other in the last few weeks. I don't think Russell enjoys having me here, underfoot, nor do I think he is over the death of his wife. How am I supposed to compete with a ghost?"

"You don't."

"Exactly."

"No, I mean… you aren't competing. You are here and have already won."

"What do you mean?"

"You are here and there is no competition. You have all the time in the world to develop a relationship to stand the test of time whereas... *not to sound cold...* her time is up. You are alive, sweet, generous, and kind, Rose—how could anyone not love you?"

"Russell doesn't," she admitted painfully, sitting across from her friend.

"You have to give him time and look for the little clues," Daisy encouraged, reaching across the table to hold Rose's hand. "Men do not think nor say the same things we do. You need to look for the deeper meaning behind their actions."

"Like what? Russell is avoiding me."

"Is he?" Daisy questioned with a knowing smile, squeezing her hand. "Or is he in town making sure no one ever treats his new wife poorly?"

"What?" Rose whispered, pulling her hand away.

"It's gossiped all over town how your husband stood up for you. I hear he made quite the scene in front of others, exclaiming that he wouldn't tolerate anyone mistreating you. In fact, I would say that if you give him a chance, you might be very pleased at how things end up."

"I *am* giving him a chance—it's Russell who is running away."

"Is he running? Or is he following his own path, beside you, at a different pace than you are used to? Take it from someone looking at your story and drawing hope from it— your husband, Russell, cares for you very much and you are blessed to have drawn his name from the envelopes when we disembarked from the train."

"Aren't you and your groom happy?"

"I'm not sure my Guillaume is capable of being happy," Daisy whispered softly, getting to her feet and looking away. Startled at the change in her friend, Rose stood too.

"Daisy... I'm sorry."

"Don't be sorry for me," she giggled nervously, but it was a dry, false laugh that didn't reach Daisy's eyes.

"All will be fine, sweet friend. I'm always happy and nothing will ever diminish that outlook on life. The sun will always shine, no matter if I am laughing or crying—so I choose to laugh. When things go wrong or it gets tough, you have to make a choice too. What will be *your* choice and what kind of impact will it have on you both?"

Rose stared at the woman, stunned by the knowledge that Daisy had just bowled her over with. Her friend was right. Everything she did was a choice. She could choose to keep reaching out to Russell, or she could lick her wounds, pout, and lose him.

"And on that bit of enlightenment I've shared? I think I shall head home to work on my own budding relationship— or lack there-of," Daisy said with a knowing smile. "My work here is done. It's up to you now, Rose."

"I thought you wanted to talk and learn more about how I make bread?"

"Yes and no," Daisy replied with a laugh. "I wanted to see your side of things and how it all was going between you two. I saw Russell in town buying you a gift. He was quite concerned about you, and suggested I come say hello because he feared that you might be lonely..."

Rose grabbed the corner of the table with her flour covered hands to keep from falling over at the simple statement. *Her husband bought her a gift and was worried she was lonely?*

Daisy continued on talking as if nothing was amiss.

"...Apparently I need to take my own advice regarding my husband and my marriage. Those that can't do, teach others... or something like that, I guess?" Daisy nodded sagely, opening the door before looking back at Rose.

"Maybe someday soon we will talk again and things will be different for the both of us? I hope and pray for that daily."

"I would like that to be true," Rose confessed honestly.

"I would as well, my friend. You must come see me soon and let me know how things work out for you."

"I promise."

"Good."

THAT EVENING, Rose waited and waited for Russell to return. She didn't know how long he was going to take before returning to the house, but she knew he was sleeping there each night and gone the next morning. Dimming the oil lamp, she waited there in the darkness, curious about how long it would take for him to show up.

It was a little eerie and strange that her husband was avoiding her, but more so that he was coming and going at all hours simply to keep from running into her.

The door opened slowly, and she heard his dejected sigh before he ever entered the room. Was it because he knew she was there? Her unspoken question was swiftly answered when he jumped, startled at her voice.

"I am sorry about yesterday," she began.

"What are you doing up this late?"

"Waiting to apologize."

"There's no reason."

"I think there is every reason," she countered. "I lost my temper, and you suffered the brunt of it. I made you dinner... and I promise it's not poisoned."

"That never entered my mind... until now," he mumbled, and Rose thought she heard amusement in his voice. Reaching forward, she turned up the wick, allowing the flame to grow slightly so she could see his face.

"I would like to say, '*I cooked your favorite*', but we barely know each other. I have no clue as to what your favorite meals actually are," she began softly, seeing the tightness to his jaw as he clenched his teeth. He was holding a wrapped package in his hand and she knew it was the surprise... that now *wasn't* a surprise because of Daisy.

"Why don't you take a seat and I'll serve up your plate."

"You don't have to stay up," Russell replied. "I don't want to bother you."

"I would prefer to have a chance to talk with you, if you don't mind the company?"

Rose watched as he hesitated for several moments before sitting down at the table. She got up and filled his plate, perching several yeast rolls on the side. Picking up a crock of butter, she walked back towards the table and set it down in front of him.

"I don't mind," he said quietly, surprising her. This was truly the first time that he actually extended a silent olive branch towards her. She would need to be very cautious to make sure he didn't retract it just as unexpectedly. Taking a seat, she poured herself some hot tea out of the kettle she'd kept warming... just in case.

"Would you like some tea?"

"I prefer whisky."

"It's very relaxing."

"So is whisky," he replied abruptly, picking up his fork.

She saw his shoulders slump slightly and hesitated. Getting up from her seat, she picked up a glass and walked over to the table, pouring him a glass and then putting a splash in her tea silently.

Rose had felt his eyes watching her and saw the corner of his lip turn upwards in a smile. That single, simple, unchecked moment made her realize that maybe Daisy was right. She needed to look for his signals of acceptance, not just the ones she imagined in her dreams.

"I made a small cake today too," she said quietly, the sounds of his fork punctuating the silence as it hit against the plate. "I found some maple syrup and cake flour hidden away. I thought I might try my hand at it. I'll cut you a piece once you are finished eating."

"Is it your birthday?"

"No, I just wanted to surprise you."

He set the fork down and looked at her.

"Why?"

Rose was confused and stared at him in the flickering lamplight. He actually looked just as bewildered as she felt. Was it so unknown, so strange, that someone would be nice towards him?

"Can't I do it because I want to make you happy? I would like us to be happy together?" she whispered painfully, reaching for his hand.

He pulled his hand away, and she expected him to get up, to run from her, but he remained seated. He didn't move in the slightest. She saw his gaze quickly drop to his plate and there was a tension to his shoulders that had gone from bad to worse.

He was ready to bolt.

She slowly retracted her hand and put it in her lap, partially to keep him from seeing the trembling. Swallowing hard, she held her breath and watched him.

Russell didn't leave.

It was an insignificant victory… and she'd definitely take it.

"You've a roll left and I'll go cut us two slices of cake," she whispered, getting to her feet. She would give him his space if he needed a moment. In looking at his face, watching his body, she realized maybe all of his bluster was because he was scared… *of her.*

She quietly hummed as she cut the warm cake, savoring the scent of the maple that she'd used to sweeten the batter. She hoped it was good, using just some basic ingredients to whip up something special. It was kind of flat around the middle and crispy at the edges, but the essence floating in the air was tantalizing. Turning back, she set a plate down in front of him and moved to take her seat… only to see the package waiting there.

"What's this?" she asked, sitting down.

"An apology."

"For what?"

"I didn't mean to make you mad yesterday," he said quietly. "I just didn't realize… well… I… never mind."

"Is it okay if I open it?" Rose asked gently, seeing that he was getting more and more agitated to where he couldn't finish what he was going to say. She didn't want him to get to a point where he burst out the door; instead, she was taking control and guiding their conversation. Instead of waiting for an answer, she simply began opening the package. Tearing the paper, she slowly pulled a yellow bonnet from the wrapping.

"Oh, Russell…" she breathed softly, turning it over in her hands before putting it on. "It's so very thoughtful and lovely. Thank you so much."

He was so quiet, so still, like if he was made of glass he was ready to splinter into a million pieces. Instead, she pulled off the bonnet and ignored him, taking a sip of her tea and wincing at the bitterness of the whisky.

"Oh, that's perfectly vile swill that you are drinking," she muttered.

"Helps you sleep," he breathed, relaxing just a bit. She obviously needed to keep him on a path where he was comfortable and felt safe. Problem was that she wanted to be on that proverbial 'path' and wasn't sure how to get there.

Taking a bite of the cake, she sighed in happiness. It was almost too sweet, but it cut the bitterness of the whisky just right.

"Tell me about your day," she instructed easily, taking another bite as if it was nothing and they were just having an ordinary conversation. "How many animals did you get? I know you go hunting quite a bit and sell the pelts. My husband, the town trapper," she replied, taking another bite.

"What is it like to be a trapper? Which animal is the easiest to catch, and what brings the most money to you? Do you ever need help? I'm a terrible shot, but I could always learn."

"I try not to use a gun, it damages the fur. I don't want to waste anything either, so I sell the meat to the butcher in town and clean the pelts myself before selling them."

"How do you do that?"

"I would rather not discuss it while we are eating," he mumbled and she glanced up in surprise, only to see that he had that soft hidden smile on his face again. He was teasing her.

"No, I suppose not," Rose said quietly, taking another bite of her cake. "I'm sure it's a disgusting tale full of blood, gore, and various entrails."

She heard him chuckle with laughter and nearly purred in happiness. If he could tease her, she could do the same! Beaming, she hefted her cup upwards and held it out towards him.

"To the start of a wonderful friendship that begins with cake," she began and held her breath as he lifted his glass and hesitated. She thought for a moment he might freeze or say something to begin an argument, but instead he tapped his glass against hers.

She noticed he didn't repeat her words like a normal toast would have occurred... *peculiar*, she mused. Instead, he shoved a big bite of his cake in his mouth and downed his whisky.

"I need to get to bed," he said in explanation.

"I do too," she replied, yawning.

He hesitated, before hurrying to his cot and facing towards the wall. Daisy's words played in her ears. Remember, it's the little things that you need to look for. Maybe he isn't running away or turning his back on you...

It was hard to stay optimistic when it sure looked to be the exact opposite.

Sighing heavily, she got to her feet and set their dishes on the wooden counter. Padding silently through the house, she heard his intake of breath only for a moment before disappearing into her room and putting herself to bed.

CHAPTER 7

"Good morning," Rose called out quickly.

She had her wrapper pulled tightly around her gown as she stood near the fireplace that bisected the living area from her room. Russell's frame nearly filled the doorway, outlining him against the sunrise off in the distance. Her heart clenched in her chest as her stomach flip-flopped wildly in her abdomen at the sight of him.

"I was just heading out," he replied. "I didn't mean to wake you."

"I wish you would have," she countered boldly with a smile, leaning on the fireplace and crossing her arms over her chest.

"I would like to have my morning cup of coffee with you and we could start the day with just a few moments together. I wouldn't feel so lonely then—and on that note- thank you for sending Daisy out to check on me. We had a lovely visit."

"I'm glad."

He hesitated, looking away from her, his hand resting on the door.

"You look pretty in the mornings when you smile," he said

quietly, and Rose felt her jaw drop open at the open admission from him. He glanced over his shoulder and nodded tightly.

"I'll be back at dusk for supper," he rushed quickly, shutting the door behind him.

Rose would have none of it!

The last time he said he would be back at dusk ended up being two months' worth of isolation because he showed up long after she'd gone to bed and disappeared before she got up. Angrily, she tugged the door open and hollered at him as he was halfway across the glen already.

"Dusk is when the sun is *setting*... not after I've gone to sleep! I will see you at *sunset!*" she yelled like a crazed woman, blushing at how uncouth it was considered doing such a thing... and smiled at his carefree laughter she heard in response.

"Yes, ma'am!" he hollered over his shoulder, raising his arm and waving.

Rose watched his figure as he disappeared into the woods and couldn't fight the burst of joy within her. Her face felt like it would a split right in two with the massive smile that blossomed at his words as she shook her head in disbelief and happiness.

This certainly was progress!

As the day went along, Rose got quite a bit of work done around the log cabin, including inspecting the cracks within the timbers to see if the chinking needed to be replaced or filled in before the snows hit hard. She could feel a draft in a few places and was concerned that it would be severely frigid, hard to keep the cabin warm, or that rodents would somehow slip inside in their own struggles to stay warm during the bitter winter storms.

She would need to focus on quite a few things before the first snow, and that included gathering up what vegetables she could. Canning, being thrifty, and smart with how they stocked up for the winter could make or break a family that was struggling to get by.

She assumed that they were poor because she hadn't seen him really purchase anything other than her bonnet, her gift. She tried to pay for the goods brought out by the nasty-tempered clerk. Yes, she wanted to make sure that they had plenty to eat... and that started with taking advantage of every moment, including this gloriously sunny day, regardless of the crisp breeze.

Gathering her basket, she trudged off into the woods with her shawl wrapped around her. There could be many treasures found, if you knew where to look for them. Mushrooms, fiddleheads, walnuts, and other foods from the earth.

It wasn't just a matter of putting food on the table because they could do hunting year-round; it was the items that made the meals special. Walnut shells could dye fabric or yarn... the meat of the nut made an amazing and filling sweet bread.

Those fiddleheads seemed to be prolific in the area closest to one creek that led out of town towards the river. She intended to blanch them so they could be stored and used in a soup or stew later. The small patch of potatoes she'd discovered quite by mistake one afternoon were pulled up quickly... along with the tree that was growing alongside of the cabin.

Kneeling down, Rose set her basket on the forest floor and grabbed her knife out of it, intending to remove some of the mushrooms she'd discovered from a recent rain. The golden caps were easy to spot against the mossy ground.

Busily, she gathered the items and froze as she heard a branch break close behind her. Ever so slowly, she turned to look over her shoulder while praying fervently that it wasn't a bear or a moose that had come upon her.

Bears she knew were dangerous... but moose were incredibly terrifying and from what she understood, unpredictable. Tales of men being killed while hunting had spread far and wide when she was a child. A great northern monster that resembled a deer was bigger than a horse, as tall as a house... and temperamental as a fishwife according to her father. She'd seen one in the far distance through the safety of the log cabin's window—and that was enough for her!

They looked to be beastly creatures!

Rose let out her breath, seeing a quite plump beaver was nearby - and he obviously had the same idea she did. He was gathering items and watching her closely, trying to determine if she was a threat to him or not.

Her smile faded as she looked upward into a pair of glossy black eyes staring back at her from the bushes. The problem was that those eyes were attached to a large brown muzzle full of razor-sharp teeth.

Getting to her feet slowly, she didn't want to antagonize the bear, but rather give herself a fighting chance at running away from him. She had a knife, and that would be no comparison against a bear.

A loud explosion sounded, causing her to jump and slap her hands over her ears as she yelped in fear, her eyes pinched shut tightly. Instantly, her hands dropped, and she patted her torso. For a moment, she was certain that she'd been shot, but as she realized that she was fine, Russell came stomping through the thicket of bushes nearby and paled.

"I nearly shot you!"

"I thought you didn't like to shoot animals?"

"I don't—but I also like drawing air in my lungs!" he

snapped. "That bear would have killed you in an instant. And why are you wearing a green dress in the middle of the forest? I never saw you until it was nearly too late."

"You should look where you are aiming," she replied primly, straightening her dress before picking up her basket. "Besides, I was gathering things for us and had just as much business being out here as you do."

"I will not argue with you…"

"Then quit huffing and puffing at me!" she retorted, losing her temper at the tone he was taking with her. One minute he was nice and seemed polite, the next he was barking angrily at everyone and everything nearby. "Besides, it's not like you care and I didn't scare off your catch, now did I?"

"Not like I… *what?*" he whispered dumbfounded, slinging his gun back over his shoulder and putting his head in both of his hands. He rubbed his face wearily, running his hands through his hair, before resting them on the back of his neck. He turned to face away from her… but only for a moment.

"You don't need to be out here by yourself," he hissed, looking and sounding very peeved and strained.

It surprised her at the pained confusion on his face just as he turned from her. He was always pushing her away or running, and it was incredibly frustrating. She barely had anyone to talk to, and the person she wanted to build a relationship with most of all—seemed to reject her.

Again.

"You had left and were gone again. What else am I to do with my time?"

"What *are* you doing anyway?" Russell questioned.

"Leaving you here to take care of that…" Rose said, pointing and waving her hand towards the bushes, looking away, but not before she noticed that his shoulders seemed to slump like he was quite resigned at having to take care of the bear.

"I'll give you your privacy to take care of that and quit bothering you—again," she said bitterly, as the imaginary walls went up around him again. Rose thought she made a breakthrough this morning, but perhaps it was her imagination.

Rose reached out to touch his shoulder and froze. She was the one making all the effort. She was the one trying. This relationship couldn't be one-sided or it would never work between them—they would never become a couple... and she would never have love if he rejected her at every turn.

She realized then that was exactly what she wanted from Russell. She wanted a future, happiness, and his heart... and he was fighting her at every turn.

She withdrew her extended hand, pulling it close to her chest as if it could stop the hurt burning within her at the realization. He was a puzzle to her, and just when she thought she had him figured out? There was yet another piece to be discovered.

Was this a lost cause, a mistake? She thought, catching her breath, waiting. The moments seemed to tick by ever so slowly, both unmoving.

"I will be home soon," Russell said heavily with a sigh.

Rose didn't answer or respond.

RUSSELL WAS HAVING a hard time coping with what had just happened.

He'd seen Rose in the woods. A beam of sunshine broke through the trees, illuminating her almost like a wood nymph or magical fairy... just as beautiful and so out of touch.

It was an idyllic scene that took his breath... almost as much as the bear he'd been tracking and taken aim towards. He'd been holding the rifle, ready to fire, when Rose had emerged.

His heart staggered, clenching in disbelief. That moment had crashed into him, causing him to hesitate as he realized that she was between him and the bear.

He'd been following the bear for a bit, knowing someone injured it using a trap. The trail of blood had been both a blessing and a curse. He didn't want to leave a wounded animal to struggle and attack, crazed with pain.

He was a hunter but believed in being humane towards the animals. He never killed for sport, but rather to put food on his table and provide an income. Russell had never condoned the gaping metal traps—they were dangerous to other hunters and deadly.

The bear had been bleeding and limping for a bit, causing him to follow it... only to see the two of them in the small clearing hidden within the trees. He nearly cried out a warning - only to see the bear's focus narrow directly on Rose as she knelt down, unaware of the dangers hidden before her.

Yanking up the gun, he held still, stepping forward slightly to take the shot.

He prayed swiftly that Rose didn't move—and that the bear didn't attack her. A wounded killer was beyond deadly. His beautiful bride would never have a way to defend herself if the bear surged forward.

It went against everything within him to level the rifle just beyond her shoulder, but he would only have the one shot. Usually when he hunted, he went for smaller creatures that were easier to carry and dispatch. Bears, moose, elk… those could be deadly if they didn't fall quickly.

His heart pounded so loudly, it thrummed between his ears, drowning out any other sounds. He never heard the bear's growl, Rose's cry of fright, nor the blast from his rifle. Instead, he saw everything move in terrifyingly slow motion before him.

The bear reared upwards, revealing its torso. Rose was moving from a kneeling position to a standing one and thankfully the bear moved in unison, allowing him the shot he so desperately needed to save her.

The smoke curled from the end of the rifle as the bear dropped, and he saw Rose's ashen face turn towards him in stunned realization. That fearful, shaken expression on her face was almost his undoing.

Jacqueline had been too good for him. She'd been taken much too soon from this world by cholera. He missed her, but Rose was different…

Rose made his blood stir unlike any other ever before. The thought of being gifted a second chance was enough to make him realize just how lucky he was. He'd been shunned all his life by everyone, but somehow he was blessed to be paired with another incredible soul to walk by his side.

She was… a miracle to him… and he couldn't let anything happen to her or he knew he would never survive it. She would take his very heart with him and the knowledge of it was staggering. That wounded bear nearly robbed him of her lovely smiles, her sharp wit, and candid tongue that always seemed to surprise him.

"I nearly shot you!" he burst out, trying to keep from yelling as the adrenaline rushed through him, combined with fear and the knowledge that he was coming to care for his new bride.

His second chance at life… and a happiness that he never imagined.

"I thought you didn't like to shoot animals?"

"I don't—but I also like drawing air in my lungs!" he snapped. "That bear would have killed you in an instant. And why are you wearing a green dress in the forest? I never saw you until it was too late."

"You should look where you are aiming," she replied primly, straightening her dress before picking up her basket. He'd never seen the basket beside her and almost cursed aloud to see the tiny knife inside. That would have done nothing towards the bear but anger it further. If she was going to be traipsing about, she'd need a rifle or something to defend herself.

He'd failed her and didn't even realize it.

"Besides, I was gathering things for us and had just as much business being out here as you do," she continued on, making Russell realize that she was still talking and he wasn't paying attention, but was absorbed in his own failures and realizations at that moment.

He had been avoiding her because he was afraid of what being with her could create. He was terrified to fall for someone that didn't return his affections and recognized now that it was a hopeless effort.

"I will not argue with you…" he said numbly.

"Then quit huffing and puffing at me!" she hollered, looking furious. "…Besides, it's not like you care and I didn't scare off your catch, now did I?"

"Not like I… *what?*" he whispered.

This was going all wrong…

Russell rubbed his face wearily, running his hands through his hair, before resting them on the back of his neck. He needed to fix this! He needed to think! Turning away from her, he spoke quietly, hoping that he could bridge the gap between them, that he seemed to be making worse and worse with each moment that passed.

"You don't need to be out here by yourself."

"You had left me once again. What else am I to do with my time?" she said aloud in disbelief and anger. That chasm between them was widening by leaps and bounds. He saw the pain in her eyes and knew he caused it.

You utter fool, he thought to himself.

"What *are* you doing anyway?"

"Leaving you here to take care of that..."

... I'm losing her before we've even had a chance, he realized, feeling the loss and more alone than ever before. He turned away so she couldn't see the tears that burned at his eyes.

"I'll give you your privacy to take care of that and quit bothering you—*again,*" Rose's voice said, painfully tight, directly behind him. He had to make this right somehow and couldn't just lose her without a fight.

"I will be home soon," Russell began unsure how to win his prickly Rose over. He turned at the silence behind him, only to see that she was already gone... in more ways than one. He watched her stiff posture as she walked away from him without turning back.

He wasn't just losing her—she was already gone...

If things were going to change, he needed to let down his guard and give this marriage a chance. Fear of being hurt, losing his memories of Jacqueline, or replacing his dearly departed wife... that had held him back.

Russell wanted a friend, a companion, and a soulmate... something he realized now he didn't have before. The spark between him and Rose was deeper than any he'd felt with Jacqueline. He'd loved her, but differently... what he felt for Rose was deeper and just as precious.

He would fight to win Rose's love or die trying...

CHAPTER 8

RUSSELL COULD NOT FOCUS AND JUST WANTED TO BE RID OF the bear, the memories, and reach out towards Rose to make amends. He was messing everything up and today was a shocking reminder that in this harsh world… he could lose her. The idea of her slipping away, being injured, or going missing before he ever had a chance to bare his soul didn't sit well at all with him.

He wanted her to smile at him, reach for him, and for them to find a common ground between them.

As he got into town, he realized that it would take more than just trying to court his wife, but rather he would need to embrace the idea that he wasn't alone anymore. He hadn't even done that with Jacqueline, he realized sadly. Rose had been so pleased with the bonnet, maybe she would like something else decidedly feminine from him? He just needed a chance with his new wife—and to not muck it up this time either. Offloading the animal, he headed straight across the way towards the milliner's shop. He saw the closed sign on the window but knew that was just a front.

Saul Bisset had been one of the men in town that received a bride as well. The man had been struggling to make ends meet as his previous wife had been the seamstress that kept the business going. Saul was a weaver and spent his time elsewhere, avoiding the shop that was once his wife's—but it wasn't easy since he lived above it.

"Saul! Open up!" Russell banged noisily.

The door opened slowly, and he stepped inside as a lamp was suddenly illuminated brightly, blinding him for a moment. He noticed Saul was holding the lamp aloft and standing right beside a woman, who took a step towards him.

"Sir? Can I help you? Is everything alright?"

"Charlotte, step back and I'll take care of him," Saul said boldly, stepping between him and the woman.

"I can speak for myself," she hissed.

Russell almost laughed at the idea of this slip of a woman taking him to task. She looked very unassuming and barely came to his chest, but there was a fierce determination in her eyes that stopped him from doing so. She reminded him of Rose—with that same forceful nature hidden within her.

"I know you are closed, but I need something... *special.*"

"We are closed," Saul said firmly, pointing at the door.

"You are Rose's new husband, aren't you?" the woman said gently, laying a hand on Saul's shoulder. "I haven't visited yet, as we've been busy with the shop. How is she?"

"She's well enough."

"What can we do for you then?"

"I need a... well... a gift."

"For what reason?" the woman named Charlotte said cannily, watching him.

It surprised Russell that she looked young, but her eyes were aged beyond her years. She might be youthful, but there was a truth to the idea of a person being an 'old soul'. She was wise, and his being here was a sign that he was trying to make amends.

"You don't have to tell me the reason or what happened," Charlotte began with a soft smile of understanding. "I am curious to know if it's a small gift you are needing... or perhaps you are needing something that shows she means something special?"

"The latter," Russel said gruffly.

"What is Rose's favorite color, Mr....?" Charlotte asked.

"Wolfe. Russell Wolfe... and I'm not sure. I know she needs something to keep her warm, and it needs to be pretty —feminine—like her," he mumbled, feeling like a fool and regretting the idea of coming here.

He should know his wife's favorite color.

Of course, Rose would want something feminine! What woman wouldn't? He would make a mental note to ask her what her favorite color was when he returned. It could be something they could talk about that could bridge the gap between them.

"Saul, could you stir the stew and I will be right up in a few?" Charlotte asked her husband, looking up at him with wide innocent eyes. Saul looked utterly smitten as he leaned down to kiss Charlotte's forehead tenderly.

Russel felt a pang of regret and jealousy.

"Do you know Rose's measurements?"

He didn't say a word, and thankfully Charlotte took the hint. She nodded, turning to walk towards the table laden with material and waved him over.

"I believe I might have just the thing," she invited with a glimmer in her eyes.

ROSE WAS beyond any coherent thought.

As the sun set in the horizon, she felt so lost, so alone, so forgotten. Her heart was breaking. She could be this miserable at home, and at least she wouldn't be alone anymore. She thought about saying that she was sorry... but what she was apologizing for - she didn't know.

She'd done nothing wrong.

A wife maintains the house, takes care of her husband, and today while walking in the woods, she was doing just that. Nothing could have prepared her for that bear, nor the fact that she'd gotten in Russell's way. Part of her wondered that if the bear had injured her, would it have bothered him? Shaking her head, she realized that question, in itself, answered so many others.

He didn't care.

She was a hassle to him.

No matter how she tried to be kind to him, it was a struggle for Russell to return the favor. He'd looked perfectly traumatized when he'd given her the bonnet, backing away from her and racing towards the cot.

What man - what *husband* - didn't consummate the marriage for months? Did he find her ugly? She knew her face was extremely angular and her nose sharp... but she had other features that had to make her endearing, didn't she?

As her mind worked, she realized that the cornbread she was making was filling the air with a somewhat heavy scent... making her realize that it was burning. Angrily, she yanked the pan out of the stove with the corner of her skirt only to protect her hand. Immediately, she dropped it as searing heat immediately scalded her palm through the material. The pan clattered to the floor as the front door opened slowly behind her.

"What?" she cried out, clenching her hand, as she saw

Russell's concerned face and it was just too much. The dam of emotions was about to break loose and she didn't want him to see her.

"I'm just doing something incredibly ignorant and foolish again…"

A sob tore from her as she turned away, the cornbread forgotten on the floor. It was only a second before she felt hands on her shoulders, turning her towards him. Stunned, she didn't move and felt herself melt as his powerful arms wound around her, rubbing her back.

Consider the emotional dam within her utterly destroyed…

Rose gave in as another sob shook her bodily. Hot, scalding tears cascaded unchecked down her face she buried against his shirt. She was embarrassed that she was crying, that everything had brought her to this moment. She was overwhelmed, painfully aware that he was here, and she was just a nuisance to him and his world.

"Shhh…," he whispered, his breath caressing her hair. "Are you hurt, or is this all because of me?"

He pulled back slightly, smoothing her hair away from her face. She tried to duck her head away, but he held fast. Each strong, large hand was on either side of her face, holding her tight. His large dark eyes searched hers silently… and she saw something there causing her breath to hitch in her chest.

"I'm so sorry, Rose," he breathed softly, leaning down to kiss her.

It was like time stood still as they both stood there together, their eyes locked. She saw the regret, the fear, and the need in those inky depths, mesmerizing her. He froze for a moment, hesitating, and she almost balked, wondering if he was toying with her or if she was dreaming. His breath caressed her lips just before they touched hers, turning her world inside out.

The sensations, the feelings, and the emotions within her felt like a burst of flames that rushes up from a roaring campfire. Everything had been growing, festering, blooming, and ratcheting up to this very second—and it all burst forth like a thunderstorm within her soul.

The softness of his lips combined with the rough whiskers on his cheeks had a devastating effect on her, making her shiver with delight and unknown passion. It must have been the same for Russell because he never moved his hands, but instead of holding her face upwards firmly to look into her eyes, those same warm hands now cradled her as if she was infinitely precious to him.

As the kiss ended, she expected him to have regrets... for him to pull away and turn from her, but that didn't happen. Instead, a miracle occurred. Russell reached for her hands, inspecting them quietly, his fingers touching her reddened palms almost in a ticklish fashion, but she knew he was checking for blisters.

"Why don't you soak your hands under the cold water and I'll clean this up," he offered politely.

"I'll get it."

"Let me help you... please," he said, causing her to look up in surprise.

She studied his face and saw the genuine concern reflected there. Nodding, she moved away and watched him pick up the pan off the floor along with the ruined corn-bread. She expected him to lash out or complain that dinner was ruined, but he acted as if it was nothing, getting more cornmeal out and dropping a dollop of lard in a fresh skillet, putting it on the stove.

"What are you doing?"

"Making hoe-cakes? Am I doing something wrong? I am a terrible cook and nearly starved to death before you arrived," he said earnestly and it was the simple wink he gave her that was her undoing.

He was actually teasing her!

Rose felt a smile tug at her lips as she watched him curiously, her hands resting within a bowl of water. They wouldn't blister, but the cool sensation mixed with a complete fascination of what was occurring right before her... this was something she couldn't pull her eyes from! She didn't want to disturb this moment, or else this perfect dream would fade from her...

Instead, she watched as he grabbed a fork, whisked an egg, mixed it all together with a few other ingredients and drizzled it in the skillet that popped with heat as the batter hit the grease.

"How are your hands?" he breathed, staring at the skillet.

"They are fine."

"Good," he replied.

The silence was punctuated with the sizzle and crackles of the grease as he flipped over one of the golden cakes. He noticed the large pot of fiddleheads that had been blanched in boiling water and were now floating in the cool water. She hadn't scooped them out yet, trying to decide what to do with them.

"Did you boil them first?"

"Yes, just to keep us from getting sick."

A grunt of approval was the only response as he flipped another cake over. He peeked under the lid of another pot and nodded silently. The man wasn't one for words, she realized, looking away from him. He'd set his things on the floor where he'd walked inside, everything happening at once.

"That's for you," he said, interrupting her thoughts. Rose

swung her eyes back at him, uncomprehending what he was alluding to. She saw a small smile tug at the corner of his lips just before he jerked his head towards the door. "That brown package over there... It's yours."

Rose looked at the package and back at him, unsure what to do. Tentatively, she pulled her hands from the water and quickly dried them on a towel as Russell fished another cake from the hot grease, putting it onto a plate. He made no moves towards her, instead putting more batter in the grease, frying up more of the simple staple. Rose knelt down and picked up the package, wincing.

Maybe she wasn't unscathed after all... her hands ached.

Pulling gently, she opened the twine and pushed back the paper, gasping. Inside was a stunning cloak that was gorgeous. The bright red color was stark against the plain earthen colors of the house and the collar lined with fur. It practically glowed against the lamplight as she pulled it from the wax paper they had wrapped it in.

Holding it up, she caught Russell's eyes to see him watching her.

He smiled tentatively, looking unsure of himself.

"What's this for?" she whispered, taken aback.

"I wanted you to have something to keep you warm when we go for walks together," he replied. "Lots of couples go on walks together and I thought the bright red would be easy to see. It would look lovely against your skin, Rose."

"You bought this for... *me?*"

"It's not for me," he chuckled lightly, grinning. He quickly cursed, turning back to the skillet, and fished out one cake from the hot lard. Setting it down on the plate with the others, she watched, holding the cloak against her, unsure of what to say or do.

This was so unexpected and touching...

Russell set down the plate on the table and walked to her

side. Without saying a word, he took the cloak from her and draped it around her shoulders. She slid her arms into the material, realizing it wasn't just some ordinary cloak but rather a fitted, floor length coat that was pleated and gathered to cover her gown as well.

Russell fastened the large silken frog knot at the throat together.

Stepping back from her, he held out his hand, showing that he wanted her to spin around. The weight of the fitted cloak was heavy, and already she could feel the warmth it would provide during the oncoming winter season.

"This is too much..." she whispered, reaching for the elaborate knot.

"Actually, it's not enough," he confessed, watching her. "I've got a lot to make up for and I want to start now. I don't know how to be a friend or a husband, and I didn't realize that before you walked into my world."

"You were married before..."

"And I think that I failed Jacqueline too," he admitted, wincing as his gaze looked away from her. "I'd like to start over, start fresh, and..."

"But we've tried that," Rose countered, feeling like a heel as she interrupted him. "When you gave me the bonnet, I thought we were starting out fresh then too?"

"I'm an idiot..."

"No..." she began, only to have him cut her off.

"Truthfully? I'm confused and scared—and I don't know how to handle all of this," he said bluntly, his eyes blazing with the painful truth.

"I've been pushed away, rejected, and then you come into my world and pick me. I don't know what to do with that. I don't know how to be the man you married because you are so different from Jacqueline. With her it was simple smiles, a matter of holding hands, and bittersweet moments that I will never get back," he said raggedly, running a hand through his hair before looking back at her.

"… But with you, it's so very different," he confessed, his voice dropping.

"You make me want to take care of you. I want to protect you, make you smile, kiss you senseless until it overcomes you with passion, and there is something inside of me that just longs to be near you… to be in the same room as you. It frightens me at how intense it is," he whispered, watching her.

"I want to be the air you breathe, the sun on your skin, and the love in your heart… and I don't know how to do it. I know if I don't try or give it my all… I'll lose you," he uttered brokenly, his dark eyes turbulent.

"…And I can't let that happen, Rose. It can't happen just because I'm too scared to put myself out there for you. All I can do is promise to try, ask you to be patient with me, and…"

Rose flew into his arms.

He grunted with the impact of their bodies as her lips crashed into his, silencing him. It only took a second for him to respond as she kissed him. His words, this very moment… it couldn't have been any more legendary than what she imagined as she lay there at night alone.

She wasn't asking for perfection from him—all she wanted was a mere chance for them to be happy. She didn't want to be shut out, only included in his life. The idea, the realization that he wanted to try to be a couple, build a relationship together, and that he felt something for her…

Well, it was more than she ever wished for.

As the kiss ended, she smiled up at him, closing her eyes at the overwhelming feelings within her and at the sheer joy she felt being gifted a chance at happiness. They could try to become friends and now that she realized that building a relationship between them was just as important to him? They could move forward... together.

"Dusk was two hours ago," she whispered, grinning.

"I'm late... for so many things," he laughed, kissing her again.

CHAPTER 9

THEY SPENT HOURS THAT EVENING TALKING TOGETHER AT THE table, just sitting there with the empty plates between them. The stew had been cold, the corn cakes barely edible, and she hadn't gotten around to doing any of the wash that so needed to be done.

It was a perfect evening.

Russell was inquisitive, asking her a plethora of questions. What was her favorite color? What made her jump at becoming a mail-order bride? What was her family like?

His questions prompted several of her own, starting with why he was so secluded out here. They were quite a-ways from the little village which made it hard to visit with the people she'd met on the train. A solitary life had never been at the top of her list, but now she realized it gave them an unexpected privacy.

"What made you choose to go with me when you drew my name?" Russell asked quietly, looking away, almost as if he was afraid to hear her answer or reasoning behind it.

"I'm a glutton for punishment, I suppose," she quipped lightly and then hesitated, lowering her voice to a whisper.

They'd broken through finally, and it was time to become friends. She wanted to tell him the truth and what had been on her mind when she'd seen him.

"Actually, there was something in you that felt like a challenge. Growing up, I never backed down from one and my parents used to get so frustrated sometimes. I thought that if you dared me to change my mind, there must be something to this…"

Rose laughed, suddenly nervous.

"I don't know why I thought that—but I did."

Russell's smile was one of admiration and respect as he watched her.

"I saw you and thought that you were full of gumption with a backbone. Life is hard out here sometimes and it takes a strong, stubborn person to get by," he admitted. "When the snow drifts reach the rooftops and we are stuck inside because of a blizzard, it takes a strong person content with whom they are, to get by."

"How did you do it alone?" she asked painfully, reaching across the table for his hand. "Before your wife, how did you get through winters like that—alone?"

"Because I had to… I hated it, but I've always been alone."

"Well, you aren't now," she said, squeezing his hand. "You'll have the grandest-pest-ever annoying you, until you race out into the night, freezing cold, and stark raving mad."

"I doubt that will happen," he replied with an amiable smile. "What do you say that we go for a walk tomorrow? I'll show you how to shoot a rifle so if you are in the woods alone, you can protect yourself."

"What makes you think I can't shoot one?" she bragged, causing his eyes to widen as he laughed.

"I guess I'll just get you your own rifle then," he conceded easily with a proud glimmer lingering in the inky depths that watched her. Russell got to his feet and Rose felt her heart hammer in her chest as he extended his hand towards her. It was getting late and even though they'd begun to build something between them, she wasn't prepared for what the marriage bed was. No one had told her, but she wasn't completely ignorant, having seen animals in the pastures or fields. She looked away when she put her hand in Russell's, ignoring the fact that her hand shook as she placed it in his.

"It's late," he whispered, "... and I would like to take my lady out for a stroll tomorrow before the weather gets too bad out."

"Russell, I...I'm not..." she stammered, feeling her heart hammer in her chest at the understanding in his expression.

He nodded tightly.

"We are still getting to know each other and I would never press myself on you. We've only just begun and have miles to go before it prepares us for that part of our marriage. I have memories to get past in my mind, and I wouldn't want to jeopardize our future in a rush to take you to bed, Rose," he explained, his face slightly flushed with embarrassment at talking about something so personal and intimate.

"I hope you don't mind if we wait until we are both ready?"

"Oh, goodness no..." she breathed in a massive sigh of relief.

"Well, you don't have to be so emphatic about it," he grunted, clearly offended as she laughed nervously, laying a hand on his arm.

"I'm glad there is no rush," she stammered, feeling her own face redden horribly with mortification. "I would rather take time to develop feelings between us before we do something so...so..."

"Scandalous, dear wife?" he teased softly, watching her.

"Exactly... well, not really, but yes!"

Russell laughed lightly, making her blush even harder, and she felt like she was strangling to get air in her lungs from where she'd held her breath nervously.

"Good night, Rose," he told her gently, smiling down at her, before dropping a soft kiss on her cheek. "I hope you have sweet dreams tonight."

"You as well, Russell," she said automatically.

"I think this is where we part," he teased, his eyes dancing as he looked pointedly to where she was clenching his shirt, the material bunched up under her fingers.

"Oh!" she exclaimed, pulling her hand off his arm and nervously smoothing the wrinkles she'd left. As she realized she was still patting the material on his arm like he was a dog or a cat, she yanked her arm backwards, linking it with her other hand behind her back.

"Sorry about that."

"It's no bother."

"I didn't mean to be mauling you."

"I assure you—you didn't maul me."

"I guess this is goodnight?"

"Rose," he smiled tenderly at her. "Go in your room, wife, and get some rest before I take off my shirt. I think doing so will make you a little more nervous than you already are."

"Oh! Yes! Alright—goodnight," she blurted out, practically dashing from the room as if temptation itself was directly behind her, waiting. She threw herself in the small chamber behind the fireplace and lay down in bed fully clothed, positively reeling from the events of the day.

They were going to make this marriage work—together!

ROSE AWOKE the next morning to sounds of someone moving about the cabin. Sitting up, she winced as her corset rubbed a raw spot on the side of her ribcage. She'd slept in it, unsure and insecure in her future. He'd not touched her yet, but the affection he'd displayed so unexpectedly yesterday, kissing her and holding her hands, had her concerned that she might awaken unexpectedly... with company.

That was not the case.

Holding herself taut, Rose almost expected yesterday to disappear in a puff of smoke... a perfect dream. She *had* just been asleep, hadn't she? What if Russell changed his mind and was getting ready to depart from the house before she awoke, once again...

Donning a clean dress quickly, she smoothed her hair and was relieved it was still in a braid so she didn't appear too disheveled. Stepping silently around the corner, she hesitated, watching.

Russell was moving about the kitchen, standing by the stove. A plate of fried ham was waiting, along with several fried eggs, and he was pouring two cups of coffee.

Two.

"Good morning," she said nervously, unmoving.

"Morning, Rose," he replied with a shy smile. "I hope I didn't wake you?"

"No. I was getting up."

"Good. Are you hungry?"

"Yes."

"I made eggs and ham... but I cooked the eggs this time," he teased, his smile widening. She winced at the memory of the meal she'd served him once, fully aware of the reference.

"I was mad."

"You had every right to be."

"I'm sorry."

"Don't apologize—it's in the past and we are looking forward, right?"

Startled, she blinked in surprise, utterly silent.

Could they have the same thoughts, the same hopes, for the future? That had been the exact same thing, she'd told herself repeatedly. She hated looking backwards, vowing to live her life with no regrets. Life was hard enough as it was… and she wanted to move past the unpleasant things, grasping with all of her might a chance at happiness.

"Yes. Moving forward always," she breathed in agreement, moving forward to take a seat at the table. Stunned, she watched him carry the two plates over, and the two steaming cups of coffee that had given her the nerve to step forward from her shelter.

"What are your plans today? Are you very busy?" he asked, shoveling several bites in his mouth and speaking between morsels. He halted, looking at her nervously.

"Is yours cooked the wrong way?"

"No," she replied, picking up her fork.

"I'm sorry. I'm starving and it smelled so good. I guess you probably think I have horrible table manners."

"Not at all," she blurted out and then smiled, looking down at her plate. "I just think maybe you might resemble your surname just now and it's amusing."

"I guess so, Mrs. Wolfe…" he teased softly.

She glanced up at him, her fork mid-air, and met his eyes. He looked so genuinely earnest and hopeful, that she couldn't help the smile that touched her own lips.

"I thought I might stay around the house today, working on chopping some more wood so we don't have to worry about it this winter. Perhaps this afternoon, we could go for a walk together?"

"I'd like that," she admitted, taking a bite. "I do have quite a bit to do today. I need to make some bread, do some laundry, and then finish clearing the garden on the side of the house."

"We have a garden?" he hesitated, looking surprised.

"Yes, we have a garden," she laughed and then hesitated. "You didn't know that?"

"I never paid attention to what Jacqueline did here, and never asked. I guess I should have," he whispered.

"It's the overgrowth on the far side of the house... that colossal mess of vines and other plants? There's still some peas, broccoli, potatoes, and other things... including a pumpkin that is tiny but thriving. It's been quite neglected, but there are still some items that can be saved."

Rose hadn't intended to make Russell feel bad or remind him of his previous wife, nor refer to how their relationship was before. Instead, she wanted to turn things around and lift the mood once again.

"Jacqueline was quite the planner and obviously well-schooled in how to take care of a home. I'm relieved that there was a garden there. Between your planning and hers, we'll do well this winter together when the snows are deep," Rose reached across the table to touch his hand.

"I didn't mention it to make you feel bad, I'm just sharing that I have quite a bit of respect for the woman you were married to before. I wouldn't have thought to start a garden, yet she had begun many sorts of vegetables that were hardy and managed to make it."

"Thank you for saying all of that."

"It's just the truth."

"I know, but it also shows you've got a big heart and that you're caring. Few people would recognize or admit that my previous wife did a good job... and I feel bad that I didn't realize it."

"You were probably busy."

"And quite ignorant of what a husband and companion should be."

"Then I guess we'll learn together, won't we?"

"I'd like that."

They finished eating, separating finally as he slung his jacket across his shoulders to head out. Rose quickly made bread, setting it aside to rise. She found a few tiny apples in storage and also baked a pie for later this evening to surprise him. She busied herself with boiling water for the laundry, grabbing her basket and a trowel, before tackling the last of the garden.

Walking outside, she couldn't help but admire the figure that Russell made as he stood there, swinging the large axe in the distance. He'd taken off his jacket, rolled up his sleeves, and was hard at work. His shirt clung to him, where his muscles pulled and strained with raw strength as he slung the axe over his shoulder with practiced ease.

Mercy... she thought silently to herself.

A pile of split logs, larger pieces, and several small bundles of kindling were in a growing pile on the ground close to him. She knew that once he was done chopping, he would haul the wood towards the house, replenishing the stack that lined the south wall of the cabin.

Rose didn't wear her beautiful coat into the garden and was glad of it as she knelt down, beginning her work. She dug up several potatoes, found a few turnips, and picked what was left of the vegetables. Yes, this would be the last harvest except for the tiny pumpkin.

She would give it a little while longer, hoping it would grow in the cooler temperatures. She would be sure to save some seeds so she could grow more next year, since the bright gourd would keep rather well with no work on her part.

Filling her basket, she got to her feet and stretched. She realized that Russell was already stacking the wood, the axe resting on the stump he'd been using to split the timbers. Looking upwards, the sun was set high in the sky, and she would need to finish up quickly if she was to be ready to go for an afternoon walk with him. The clothes had been soaking in the boiling water and would be ready to hang after a good scrubbing too. There was so much still to do!

Wincing, she quickly hurried, hauling the heavy basket towards the house and setting it by the stoop where the tin tub sat cooling. Grabbing a board, she quickly scrubbed the material and hung it on the line. She emptied the tub, turning it over in the grass to dry.

Picking up the basket, she headed inside. The potatoes went in a bin she'd found in the pantry, along with the turnips. Broccoli would need to be cooked or eaten soon. The peas could be shelled and dried, making a savory soup later.

"Rose?" Russell's voice interrupted her just as she finished emptying the basket of all the treasures she'd harvested. "Can I help with anything or will you be finished soon?"

"No, no. I'm going to be ready in a moment," she quickly said, looking away as she saw that she had smudges on her dress and several wisps of her hair had freed from her braid. "I'm a mess and I…"

"You look lovely," he said, almost directly behind her.

Rose glanced up at him in surprise and noticed the longing in his face. He reached forward, tucking one of the errant curls behind her ear, smiling softly at her. There was a raw warmth in his gaze that made her hesitate from moving away.

"You look beautiful," he whispered. "I'm a very lucky man."

"I look quite a mess," she countered nervously.

"Never…" he breathed, leaning down slowly towards her. "May I kiss you or shall I wait until later?"

"What's happening later?" she whispered, staring up at him.

"Nothing," he confessed with an endearing, lopsided

smile. "I just plan on kissing my gorgeous bride every day, at least once, so she knows I'm thinking of her and that you are always on my mind."

"Oh," she sighed in response, as if that single word answered every question, melting visibly at his words. Instead of teasing her or continuing the banter between them, he closed the distance between them, their lips touching.

That was the one thing she adored about this change in him, how real everything seemed to be between them once he'd let her in, relinquishing his protective walls he'd built around himself. His lips touched hers, almost hesitating, as if to give her a chance to back away. When she didn't, the pressure was encouraging, coaxing her to kiss him back silently. His palms cradled her neck, his fingers touching the nape of her hair, creating goosebumps on her skin.

Russell was tender, sweet, and just what she needed in a husband to counter the wildness in her soul with no confrontation. This soft core was hidden under such a handsome gruff exterior and she was even more prized that she could witness such an intimate, revealing side of him.

"I like this," she whispered softly as their kiss broke, her hands touching his chest, clenching his shirt to keep her knees from collapsing underneath her.

"I adore this," he countered, kissing her again.

This time, it was slightly different.

The sweet tenderness that had been there before between them was fizzling and growing into something exponentially more. His hands moved from the back of her neck to her back, pulling her even closer to him, resting at the base of her spine. Her own hands released the fabric of his shirt, reaching up to run her fingers through his hair as her arms wrapped around his shoulders.

Rose found that kissing Russell was heady and eye-opening. There was a wild untapped passion flaring to life between them. Gasping, she pulled herself free and clenched the framework of the pantry to keep from falling. Her legs felt weak and her hands were trembling with the sensations coursing through her.

Russell suddenly cleared his throat and ran his hand along the back of his neck nervously, the other hand resting on his hip, as he looked away. She saw he looked just as surprised as she felt.

"I'll… ah… I will give you some time to get ready," he stammered. "I think I need some air and a second to… ah… I'll be outside."

This time, she didn't feel hurt or rejected when he turned to walk outside without another word. He was running, but this time it was different.

Now she understood the unspoken emotions racing through them both, even if she couldn't comprehend what it would mean in the long run for the two of them. Instead of being upset that he was stepping away from her? She touched her lips with her trembling fingers… and smiled with all the knowledge of Eve that her husband was feeling desire for her in return.

ROSE TOOK MORE than a few minutes to change her dress, brush out her hair, forgoing the braid. She wanted to look as pretty and feminine as possible since he was making an effort to court her. She wanted to respond in kind, attempting to look nice for him.

She donned the stunning red fitted cloak and smiled to herself. It was quite warm and felt almost like she was buttoning an outer gown because of the darts built into the fabric, causing it to flare in just the right places. It was breathtaking, and her husband obviously thought highly of her to get her such an extravagant gift that would be worn for years to come.

Pinching her cheeks and taking one last look at herself in the small mirror, Rose stepped forward towards the door, excited about their outing. As she opened the door, she saw him standing with his back towards the house. The iron hinge gave a small tell-tale creak, and she saw him turn to look at her. The smile on his face was telling.

Without a word, he crossed the yard and held out his hand.

"My lady?"

"Husband," she replied breathlessly, laying her hand in his. She almost expected him to give her his arm as they walked, but he made no move to release her hand. Instead, he laced his fingers with hers.

"Do you mind?"

"Not at all," she answered shyly.

Holding his hand, or touching him, was quickly growing to be one of her favorite things. She loved the differences between them. His hands were firm, warm, callused and decidedly masculine, making her own hands feel quite delicate regardless of her jagged nails and roughness.

"I'd like to show you something, if you are up for it? It's a little way from here and closer to the river," he began, looking upwards. "It's a little late in the afternoon, but I should have you back by dusk."

"Your version of dusk or mine?" she taunted, smiling shyly.

"Definitely yours," he chuckled, sharing a glance. "Although, as your husband, I can keep you out late and unchaperoned without fear of your reputation."

"Scandalous, sir!" she replied with mock concern.

"I know," he teased. "Downright wicked of me, isn't it?"

"It certainly is."

"Shall I take you back?"

"Never," she grinned.

Russell winked at her before they both began laughing at the easy banter between them. Walking, she noticed that he seemed almost nervous as he kept going, stealing glances at her occasionally when he thought she wasn't looking.

How could she *not* look at him?

Everything about him fascinated her.

Those bittersweet, but surprisingly rare, smiles that touched her soul. The way he cocked his head curiously, and his eyes danced with laughter, as he listened to some odd comment she had to make... The warmth in his gaze, like he was seeing her for the first time—every time. He had a quick wit, a boyish enthusiasm, a sensitive soul hidden away, and only revealed this aspect of his personality to her alone.

While she loved a challenge, this mysterious man was quickly capturing her heart with the many facets of his personality. He kept her on her toes and the intangible game between them seemed to always be afoot. She yearned for the next surprise, the next unexpected revelation... and because of this chameleon of a man who kept drawing her in?

Rose was falling in love with her husband.

He drew to a stop and hesitated, observing her face. Looking ahead, she could see a stone wall not too far away, an overlook just beyond it in the distance. The river was ahead, but far enough away to allow the trees to create a windbreak. The surrounding area was cleared meticulously and with care.

"Where are we?" she asked quietly, very confused.

"We are still on our land," he began, releasing her hand and stepping back. "Feel free to look around."

She stepped forward and realized that the enormous stone wall that lay ahead of them, while unfinished, was more than just a wall. It was the outer frame of a home! Stunned, she walked in the doorway that was angled away from the riverfront to protect it from the breeze.

Massive, smoothed river rocks had been stacked meticulously over time, building this home. She saw the gigantic fireplace inside was untouched and the chimney was still a work in progress. There were several rooms to this home, not just the one open area. The rooms were tiny, and the windows were barely framed in within a few of them. A pump was installed to make sure there was water at all times, along with the framing of a large pantry.

"Do you like it?"

"I don't understand…" Rose stammered, turning towards Russell. He stood there next to the fireplace, his eyes watching her sharply. "What is this place? Where are we?"

"I had nothing growing up and always dreamt of having a home, something special, that I could pass down to my children. When Jacqueline died, I thought for sure that my future had died with her…" he admitted quietly.

"I started building this place about two months before Jacqueline died and didn't touch it again until recently."

"You did?"

He nodded.

"I didn't know what to do anymore when you suddenly appeared. I didn't ask for a wife and knew I'd been given one regardless, so I threw myself into my hopes and dreams… wishing for a future. I wasn't avoiding you, Rose," he grimaced.

"I was working on me…"

Stunned, she felt her heart hammer in her chest at his words, trying her best to comprehend this moment as it played out before her. Looking around, she saw that some mixture between the rocks looked fresh and that there was still so much to do on the house before it would be finished.

"I felt guilty that the house I'd been building for my future with my wife, now belonged to a different woman...," he admitted quietly, taking a deep breath. A faint puff of white drifted up between them as fat snowflakes fell all around them, within the house frame that lacked a roof above them.

"...But then I realized that even though I'd made mistakes, it didn't change things. I still want to be able to pass down a part of me, a part of myself, a part of something I've made to others. I can only hope we would pass it to family, but that all starts with a chance—and with you."

He smiled, looking particularly nervous and hopeful, blinking as the snow dusted his hair and caught on his eyelashes.

"I know that we are just now getting to know each other —but I felt that there was no better way to know me, than to share my fondest wish. I want to finish our home, to make it full of laughter and love someday, and to have a life full of precious moments where you serve me raw eggs when I make you mad..." he laughed softly, giving her an endearing smile that nearly broke her heart as tears burned at her eyes.

This gorgeous, gruff man was baring his soul to her in a place that meant the most to him. She wanted to be a part of his life and he'd guided her to the very heart of who he was... asking her to join his side instead of assuming she would be there.

"I want us to not only finish this house together—but I want to make it a home, our home, with you, Rose."

"Russell...," she said thickly, knowing that nothing she would ever say could compare to how wonderful his words were to her. For a girl that never fit in, ran away from every-thing, and felt like she didn't have a home to return to... he was asking her to be a part of his world - and he didn't have to.

He wanted to!

"You don't have to say anything," he stammered, looking nervous as could be. She recognized the signs as he ran his fingers through his hair and rested his hand on the back of his neck. He always seemed to do that when he was deep in thought, she realized.

"I just wanted you to see this place, to see if there were any changes you wanted to make before I got too far in the construction of it," Russell mumbled. "If you don't like it, we can start..."

"I love it," Rose interrupted, taking a step towards him.

His eyes shot upwards to her, and she saw the insecurity in his depths. He knew that the house wasn't perfect, but the bigger picture was that he made it, for his future, for a family someday that he craved more than anything. Acknowledging that they would have such a thing between them meant that she was accepting him.

"Are you... *sure?*" he whispered. There was so much pain, so much need in his broken words. Her hands clenched together over her heart, and she felt like it would burst at the emotions within her.

"I'm certain that I absolutely love it," she breathed raggedly, the words catching in her throat as she stepped closer to him, staring in his eyes.

"Russell, it's more perfect than anything I could have dreamed of—and I cannot imagine anything more wonderful than taking on something so beautiful and passing it down... to our children someday."

"I will always be kind to you, Rose."

"And I would expect you to be," she quipped with a smile as a tear rolled down her cheek. "You can get ill from eating that much raw food, my husband."

He laughed thickly and wiped his eyes as he took her hands and lay them over his heart. His eyes searched hers, a window to his soul, and she was more than ready to make the leap of faith he was asking of her.

"I don't deserve you."

"But you are trapped with me," she countered softly.

"Thank God..." he said breathlessly, pulling her into his arms.

His lips crashed down on hers with such an intensity that she knew he was feeling as much as she was. They were both making a promise to each other, a pact, to give them both a future they never thought they would ever have. He was showing her everything he had to give and hoping she would recognize it for what it was.

His heart.

He might not have said the words, but it was there, none-theless.

In the middle of the snowy wonderland surrounding them, within the home they would have someday, a lonely man kissed the woman he loved, sealing this promise between them.

Rose drew a ragged breath and stared up into his dark eyes that were full of a future she never imagined or dreamed of.

"I love you," she whispered earnestly.

Rose was so thankful to have made the bravest, most terrifying life-altering decision in her life... becoming a mail-order bride, taking a chance on life, love, happiness, and marriage, in the wilds of Canada.

CHAPTER 10

A week later...

"Open the door! OPEN UP NOW!"

A hand pounded on the front door of their log cabin, rousing the sleeping couple from the bed that they lay in. Rose glanced at her husband, still stunned by the ferocity of emotions that tore through her at a single smile.

She loved him with every fiber of her being and was so grateful that she'd drawn his letter. The idea that something, anything, could have gone wrong was terrifying, and she hoped the others had just as much luck as Fate had blessed her with...

Unfortunately, the answer to that question was currently pounding on the door.

"Stay here, love," Russell said tenderly.

"No, I'm getting up," she countered.

"You never listen to me..."

"And you love me despite how contrary I am."

"You're darn right, I do!" he grinned, yanking on a shirt.

The pounding became even louder and more rampant,

causing the couple to look at each other in alarm. Something was seriously wrong!

"Get the rifle, honey."

"You get it! I recognize that voice," Rose said in dawning horror.

She ran carelessly toward the front door of the cabin, pulling her robe about her. She opened the door only to see a bedraggled woman collapse within the doorway, quickly kicking it shut emphatically.

"Lock the confounded door, Rose!" Belle hollered painfully, sounding almost as if she was strangling to get the words out of her out of sheer disbelief, her eyes glassy with tears.

"What's going on?"

"Just bar the door, please? I need to hide!"

"What in tarnation is happening?"

"Did you bring trouble to our door?" Russell said angrily, grabbing Rose by the arm and pulling her behind him. Belle was getting up from the floor, dusting herself off before the couple.

"I just need a place to lie low for a while."

"Why?"

"Don't worry about it," Belle responded vaguely, peering out the window for a second before looking at them both. The woman before them looked utterly terrified and alarmed.

"I'm just not ready."

"Ready for what?" Rose and Russell chirped out at the same time, looking at each other. Her husband checked the rifle to make sure they loaded it, in order to be certain that they were prepared for whatever imagined or real nightmares were headed in their very direction.

Belle's voice rang out in a wail full of anger and disbelief.

"To meet my Maker! They are coming to *hang* me, Rose!"

Sometimes love can't be explained or defined...

Oliver Anders always wanted to find love, but felt shunned and embarrassed by his disfigurement. He couldn't help how he looked, the scars a brutal reminder of the fire so long ago that left him alone and unwanted. Stunned and mortified, Oliver doesn't know how long he can hide away in his own home when a strange woman arrives on his doorstep, claiming to be his bride.

Penelope Greene was tired of being rejected and criticized. She'd had enough of society and wanted a place to hide away, jumping at the chance to lose herself in Lore Valley. When she arrives and discovers that her promised husband is the town pariah and supposedly horrific to look upon, but that sounds like a perfect chance to be left alone.

Can the shadows that hide her husband's face, keep her secret for very long? Will a gentle, unexpected friendship turn into something more, a genuine love that is unexpected, but definitely magical?

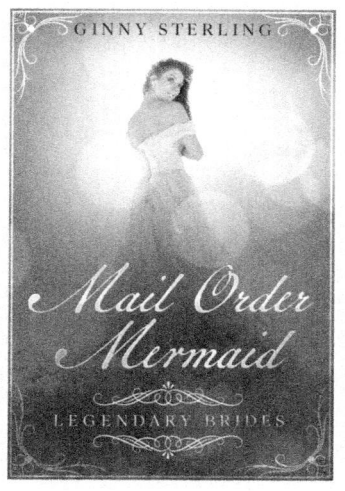

GINNY STERLING

Mail Order Miracle

LEGENDARY BRIDES

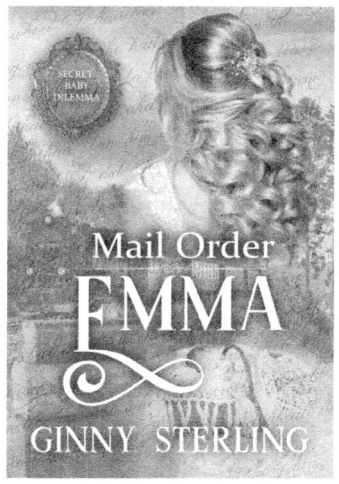

Emma Wainwright didn't believe in love.

Love was a matter of superfluous chemical reactions within the body that certain environmental influences exacerbated—or so her former scientist husband claimed. Until those outside influences, resulted in a chain reaction of unexpected and epic proportions, toppling her world. Now alone, penniless, and undeniably pregnant, the bookish bluestocking sets out to tackle her most fascinating experiment of all—dealing with her new husband, William.

William 'Willie' Thomas barely understood the language his new bride was speaking, as she stood before him, spouting out all these fancy words that were even mightier than her outstretched belly. He comprehended now what she'd meant in her letter, claiming she was *'incubating'* and *'expanding'*—but why couldn't she just spit out the truth? The new teacher in town, his bride, was extremely pregnant!

Can William's prized brutish strength in the silver mines of Nevada even compare to the knowledge his wife kept spouting everywhere?

Could two opposites come together despite their differences, finding a common ground between them? Will they be able to grow as a couple during the most obvious, impending, glorious changes coming soon within their lives?

AN AGENT FOR CLEMENTINE

Hidden identities, an infamous robbery, and a sudden marriage make for one sweet & tender adventure!

Clementine Fenton was betrothed for years to a man she'd never met, pushing off the nuptials for as long as possible. When her family goes behind her back and she discovers that her marriage is impending – she makes a break for it! Running away to join the Pinkerton Agency, she'd longed for a life of adventure and independence.

Jericho Buchannan knew this day was coming and dreaded it with every fiber in his being – he was going to be shackled into a loveless marriage with a woman he'd never seen before. He was at the precipice of his new career as an agent, something his father couldn't understand. Jericho knew his duty was to take over the family business, but yearned for a last hurrah before settling down.

ABOUT THE AUTHOR

Ginny Sterling is an avid romance writer. She lives to tell sweet, inspirational, tender tales that tug at the heart- leaving the reader smiling, laughing or crying. She favors writing western or contemporary books - several of which- are included in The Lawkeepers Series, Disaster City Search & Rescue, Legendary Brides, and her own series Healing Hearts .

Printed in Great Britain
by Amazon